QUARTET

QUARTET

Jean Rhys

> . . . *Beware*
> *Of good Samaritans — walk to the right*
> *Or hide thee by the roadside out of sight*
> *Or greet them with the smile that villains wear.*
>   R. C. Dunning

VINTAGE BOOKS
A Division of Random House / New York

FIRST VINTAGE BOOKS EDITION, September 1974

All rights reserved. Published in the United States by Random House, Inc., New York. Published by arrangement with Harper & Row, Publishers, Inc. First published in 1928 in Great Britain by Chatto and Windus under the title *Postures*.

Library of Congress Cataloging in Publication Data

Rhys, Jean.
   Quartet.
   First published in London in 1928 under title: Postures.
   Reprint of the 1969 ed. published by Deutsch, London.
   I. Title.
PZ3R3494Qu10   [PR6035.H96]   823'.9'12   78-8114
ISBN 0-394-71319-2

Manufactured in the United States of America

I

IT WAS ABOUT half-past five on an October afternoon
when Marya Zelli came out of the Café Lavenue, which is a
dignified and comparatively expensive establishment on the
Boulevard du Montparnasse. She had been sitting there for
nearly an hour and a half, and during that time she had
drunk two glasses of black coffee, smoked six caporal
cigarettes and read the week's *Candide*.

Marya was a blonde girl, not very tall, slender-waisted.
Her face was short, high cheek-boned, full-lipped; her long
eyes slanted upwards towards the temples and were gentle
and oddly remote in expression. Often on the Boulevards
St Michel and Montparnasse shabby youths would glide up
to her and address her hopefully in unknown and spitting
tongues. When they were very shabby she would smile in a
distant manner and answer in English:

'I'm very sorry; I don't understand what you are saying.'

She crossed the boulevard and turned down the Rue de
Rennes. As she walked along she was thinking: 'This street
is very like the Tottenham Court Road – own sister to the
Tottenham Court Road.'

The idea depressed her, and to distract herself she stopped
to look at a red felt hat in a shop window. Someone behind
her said:

'Hello, Madame Zelli, what are you doing in this part of
the world?'

Miss Esther De Solla, tall, gaunt, broad-shouldered, stood looking downwards at her with a protective expression. When Marya answered: 'Hello! Nothing. I was feeling melancholy, to tell you the truth,' she proposed:

'Come along to my studio for a bit.'

Miss De Solla, who was a painter and ascetic to the point of fanaticism, lived in a street at the back of the Lion de Belfort. Her studio was hidden behind a grim building where the housewives of the neighbourhood came to wash their clothes. It was a peaceful place, white-walled, smelling strongly of decayed vegetables. The artist explained that a *marchande des quatre saisons* kept her stock in the courtyard, and that as the woman was the concierge's sister-in-law, complaints were useless.

'Though the smell's pretty awful sometimes. Sit near the stove. It's cold today.'

She opened a massive cupboard and produced a bottle of gin, another of vermouth, two glasses and a cardboard case containing drawings.

'I bought these this morning. What do you think of them?'

Marya, helped by the alcohol, realized that the drawings were beautiful. Groups of women. Masses of flesh arranged to form intricate and absorbing patterns.

'That man's a Hungarian,' explained Miss De Solla. 'He's just over the way in the house where Trotzky used to live. He's a discovery of Heidler's. You know Heidler, the English picture-dealer man, of course.'

Marya answered: 'I don't know any of the English people in Paris.'

'Don't you?' said Miss De Solla, shocked. Then she added hastily: 'How perfectly lovely for you!'

6

'D'you think so?' asked Marya dubiously.

Miss De Solla assured her that it was.

'I do think that one ought to make an effort to get away from the Anglo-Saxons in Paris, or what on earth is the good of being here at all? And it isn't an easy thing to do, either. Not easy for a woman, anyhow. But, of course, your husband's French, isn't he?'

'No,' said Marya. 'He's a Pole.'

The other looked across at her and thought: 'Is she really married to the Zelli man, I wonder? She's a decorative little person – decorative but strangely pathetic. I must get her to sit to me.'

She began to argue that there was something unreal about most English people.

'They touch life with gloves on. They're pretending about something all the time. Pretending quite nice and decent things, of course. But still . . .'

'Everybody pretends,' Marya was thinking. 'French people pretend every bit as much, only about different things and not so obviously. She'll know that when she's been here as long as I have.'

'As long as I have.' The four years she had spent in Paris seemed to stretch into infinity.

'English people . . .' continued Miss De Solla in a dogmatic voice.

The drone of a concertina sounded from the courtyard of the studio. The man was really trying to play 'Yes, we have no bananas'. But it was an unrecognizable version, and listening to it gave Marya the same feeling of melancholy pleasure as she had when walking along the shadowed side of one of those narrow streets full of shabby *parfumeries*, second-hand book-stalls, cheap hat-shops, bars frequented by gaily-painted ladies and loud-voiced men, midwives' premises . . .

Montparnasse was full of these streets and they were often inordinately long. You could walk for hours. The Rue Vaugirard, for instance. Marya had never yet managed to reach the end of the Rue Vaugirard, which was a very respectable thoroughfare on the whole. But if you went far enough towards Grenelle and then turned down side streets . . .

Only the day before she had discovered, in this way, a most attractive restaurant. There was no *patronne*, but the *patron* was beautifully made up. Crimson was where crimson should be, and rose-colour where rose-colour. He talked with a lisp. The room was full of men in caps who bawled intimacies at each other; a gramophone played without ceasing; a beautiful white dog under the counter, which everybody called Zaza and threw bones to, barked madly.

But Stephan objected with violence to these wanderings in sordid streets. And though Marya considered that he was extremely inconsistent, she generally gave way to his inconsistencies and spent hours alone in the bedroom of the Hôtel de l'Univers. Not that she objected to solitude. Quite the contrary. She had books, thank Heaven, quantities of books. All sorts of books.

Still, there were moments when she realized that her existence, though delightful, was haphazard. It lacked, as it were, solidity; it lacked the necessary fixed background. A bedroom, balcony and *cabinet de toilette* in a cheap Montmartre hotel cannot possibly be called a solid background.

Miss De Solla, who had by this time pretty well exhausted her fascinating subject, stopped talking.

Marya said: 'Yes, but it's pretty lonely, not knowing any English people.'

'Well,' Miss De Solla answered, 'if that's what you're pining for. What are you doing this evening? Come along to Lefranc's and meet the Heidlers. You must have heard of Heidler.'

'Never.'

'Hugh Heidler?' protested Miss De Solla.

She proceeded to explain Mr Heidler, who was a very important person in his way, it seemed. He made discoveries; he helped the young men, he had a flair.

'I believe they intend to settle in France for good now – Provence in the winter and Montparnasse for the rest of the year – you know the sort of thing. He's had a kind of nervous breakdown. Of course, people say—'

Miss De Solla stopped.

'I like Mrs Heidler anyway; she's a very sensible woman; no nonsense there. She's one of the few people in Montparnasse whom I do like. Most of them . . . But abuse isn't any good, and it's better to be clean than kind.'

'Much better!' agreed Marya.

'Not that they are mad on baths or nailbrushes, either,' said the other. 'Never mind.' She got up and lit a cigarette. 'Mrs Heidler paints, too. It's pretty awful to think of the hundreds of women round here painting away, and all that, isn't it?'

She looked round her austere studio, and the Jewess's hunger for the softness and warmth of life was naked in her eyes.

'Well,' said Marya, 'I'd like to come, but I must telephone to Stephan, to my husband. Where can I telephone from?'

'From the Café Buffalo. Wait a minute, I've got to stand on a chair to put my gas out. My shark of a landlady won't put in electric light. Mind you, I'm fond of this place, though the smell is really awful sometimes. That head over there doesn't look so bad in this light, does it?' said Miss De Solla, wistfully.

*

Lefranc's is a small restaurant half-way up the Boulevard du Montparnasse. It is much frequented by the Anglo-Saxons of the quarter, and by a meagre sprinkling of Scandinavians and Dutch.

The *patron* is provincial and affable. The *patronne*, who sits beaming behind the counter, possesses a mildy robust expression and the figure and coiffure of the nineties; her waist goes in, her hips come out, her long black hair is coiled into a smooth bun on the top of her round head. She is very restful to the tired eye.

The Heidlers were sitting at a table at the end of the room.

'Good evening,' said Mrs Heidler in the voice of a well-educated young male. Her expression was non-committal.

'*Encore deux vermouths-cassis!*' said Mr Heidler to the waitress.

They were fresh, sturdy people. Mr Heidler, indeed, was so very sturdy that it was difficult to imagine him suffering from a nervous breakdown of any kind whatever. He looked as if nothing could break him down. He was a tall, fair man of perhaps forty-five. His shoulders were tremendous, his nose arrogant, his hands short, broad and so plump that the knuckles were dimpled. The wooden expression of his face was carefully striven for. His eyes were light blue and intelligent, but with a curious underlying expression of obtuseness – even of brutality.

'I expect he's awfully fussy,' thought Marya.

Mrs Heidler was a good deal younger than her husband, plump and dark, country with a careful dash of Chelsea, and wore with assurance a drooping felt hat which entirely hid the upper part of her face. She sat in silence for some time listening to Miss De Solla's conversation about the dearth of studios, and then suddenly remarked to Marya:

'H. J. and I have quite made up our minds that eating is the greatest pleasure in life. Well, I mean, it is, isn't it? At any rate, it's one of the few pleasures that never let you down.'

Her eyes were beautiful, clearly brown, the long lashes curving upwards, but there was a suspicious, almost a deadened look in them.

'I'm a well-behaved young woman,' they said, 'and you're not going to catch me out, so don't think it.' Or perhaps, thought Marya, she's just thoroughly enjoying her pilaff.

Miss De Solla, looking more ascetic than ever, agreed that eating was jolly. They discussed eating, cooking, England and, finally, Marya, whom they spoke of in the third person as if she were a strange animal or at any rate a strayed animal – one not quite of the fold.

*

'But you are English – or aren't you?' asked Heidler.

He was walking along the boulevard by her side, his head carefully thrown back.

Marya assured him that she was. 'But I left England four years ago.'

He asked: 'And you've been all the time in Paris?' Then, without waiting for her to answer, he added fussily: 'Where have Lois and Miss De Solla got to? Oh, there they are! I'll just go and see if Guy is in here, Lois.'

He disappeared into the Café du Dôme.

'It's a dreadful place, isn't it?' said Mrs Heidler.

Marya, looking through the door at the mournful and tightly packed assembly, agreed that it was rather dreadful.

Heidler emerged, puffing slightly, and announced in a worried tone:

'He's not here. We'll sit on the terrace and wait for him.'

The terrace was empty and cold, but without argument they all sat down and ordered coffee and liqueur brandies.

Marya, who was beginning to shiver, drank her brandy and found herself staring eagerly and curiously at Mrs Heidler.

A strong, dark woman, her body would be duskily solid like her face. There was something of the earth about her, something of the peasant. Her mouth was large and thick-lipped, but not insensitive, and she had an odd habit of wincing when Heidler spoke to her sharply. A tremor would screw up one side of her face so that for an instant she looked like a hurt animal.

'I bet that man is a bit of a brute sometimes,' thought

Marya. And as she thought it, she felt his hand lying heavily on her knee.

He looked kind, peaceful and exceedingly healthy. His light, calm eyes searched the faces of the people passing on the Boulevard Montparnasse, and his huge hand lay possessively, heavy as lead, on her knee.

Ridiculous sort of thing to do. Ridiculous, not frightening. Why frightening?

She made a cautious but decided movement and the hand was withdrawn.

'It's very cold here,' said Heidler in his gentle voice. 'Let's go on to the Select Bar, shall we?'

*

At a little after midnight Marya got back to the Hôtel de l'Univers, Rue Cauchois. She mounted five flights of steep, uncarpeted stairs, felt her way along an unlighted passage, flung her bedroom door open and embraced her husband violently. He looked so thin after the well-fed Heidlers.

'*Tiens*, *Mado*,' he said. 'You're very late.'

The room was large and low-ceilinged, the striped wall-paper faded to inoffensiveness. A huge dark wardrobe faced a huge dark bed. The rest of the furniture shrank away into corners, battered and apologetic. A narrow door on the left led into a small, very dark dressing-room. There was no carpet on the floor.

'I've just this minute got back,' remarked Stephan.

Marya said: 'Well, was everything all right?' And when he answered, 'Yes,' she asked no further questions.

Stephan disliked being questioned and, when closely

pressed, he lied. He just lied. Not plausibly or craftily, but impatiently and absent-mindedly. So Marya had long ago stopped questioning. For she was reckless, lazy, a vagabond by nature, and for the first time in her life she was very near to being happy.

2

MARYA, YOU MUST understand, had not been suddenly and ruthlessly transplanted from solid comfort to the hazards of Montmartre. Nothing like that. Truth to say, she was used to a lack of solidity and of fixed backgrounds.

Before her marriage she had spent several years as a member of Mr Albert Prance's No. 1 touring company. An odd life. Morose landladies, boiled onion suppers. Bottles of gin in the dressing-room. Perpetual manicuring of one's nails in the Sunday train. Perpetual discussions about men. ('Swine, deary, swine.') The chorus knew all about men, judged them with a rapid and terrible accuracy.

Marya had longed to play a glittering part – she was nineteen then – against the sombre and wonderful background of London. She had visited a theatrical agent; she had sung – something – anything – in a quavering voice, and the agent, a stout and weary gentleman, had run his eyes upwards and downwards and remarked in a hopeless voice: 'Well, you're no Tetrazzini, are you, deary? Never mind, do a few steps.'

She had done a few steps. The stout gentleman had glanced at another gentleman standing behind the piano, who was, it seemed, Mr Albert Prance's manager. Both nodded slightly. A contract was produced. The thing was done.

'Miss – I say, what d'you call yourself? – Miss Marya Hughes, hereinafter called the artist.'

Clause 28: no play, no pay.

The next day she attended her first rehearsal and listened to the musical director bawling, with a resigned expression· 'Sopranos on my right, contraltos on my left.'

Mr Albert Prance himself had a curved nose, a large stomach and a long black moustache. He watched the rehearsals and would occasionally make a short speech. Something like this:

'Ladies and gentlemen. This play wants guts!'

He terrified Marya; her knees shook whenever he came anywhere near her.

Sometimes she would reflect that the way she had been left to all this was astonishing, even alarming. When she had pointed out that, without expensive preliminaries, she would be earning her own living, everybody had stopped protesting and had agreed that this was a good argument. A very good argument indeed. For Marya's relatives, though respectable people, presentable people (one might even go so far as to say quite good people), were poverty-stricken and poverty is the cause of many compromises.

There she was and there she stayed. Gradually passivity replaced her early adventurousness. She learned, after long and painstaking effort, to talk like a chorus girl, to dress like a chorus girl and to think like a chorus girl – up to a point. Beyond that point she remained apart, lonely, frightened of her loneliness, resenting it passionately. She grew thin. She began to live her hard and monotonous life very mechanically and listlessly.

A vague procession of towns all exactly alike, a vague procession of men also exactly alike. One can drift like that for a long time, she found, carefully hiding the fact that this wasn't what one had expected of life. Not in the very least.

At twenty-four she imagined with dread that she was growing old. Then, during a period of unemployment spent in London, she met Monsieur Stephan Zelli.

He was a short, slim, supple young man of thirty-three or four, with very quick, bright brown eyes and an eager but secretive expression. He spoke English fairly well in a harsh voice and (when he was nervous) with an American accent.

He told Marya that he was of Polish nationality, that he lived in Paris, that he considered her beautiful and wished to marry her. Also that he was a *commissionaire d'objets d'art*.

'Oh, you sell pictures,' she said.

'Pictures and other things.'

*

Marya, who had painfully learnt a certain amount of caution, told herself that this stranger and alien was probably a bad lot. But she felt strangely peaceful when she was with him, as if life were not such an extraordinary muddle after all, as if he were telling her: 'Now then, look here, I know all about you. I know you far better than you know yourself. I know why you aren't happy. I can make you happy.'

And he was so sure of himself, so definite, with such a clean-cut mind. It was a hard mind, perhaps, disconcertingly and disquietingly sceptical. But at any rate it didn't bulge out in all sorts of unexpected places. Most people hesitated. They fumbled. They were so full of reticences and prejudices and uncertainties and spites and shames, that there was no getting anywhere at all. One felt after a time a blankness and a jar – like trying to walk up a step that wasn't there. But, good or bad, there Monsieur Zelli was. Definite. A person. He criticized her clothes with authority and this enchanted her. He told her that her arms were too thin, that she had a Slav type and a pretty silhouette, that if she were happy and petted she would become charming. Happy, petted, charming – these are magical words. And the man knew what he was talking about, Marya could see that.

As to Monsieur Zelli, he drew his own conclusions from her air of fatigue, disillusion and extreme youth, her shadowed eyes, her pathetic and unconscious lapses into helplessness. But he was without bourgeois prejudices, or he imagined that he was, and he had all his life acted on impulse, though always in a careful and businesslike manner.

It was the end of a luncheon in Soho. Marya finished smoking her cigarette and remarked:

'You know I haven't got any money, not a thing, not a cent.'

She said this because, when he had leaned forward with the lighted match, he had reminded her of China Audley's violinist.

China, also one of Mr Prance's discoveries, was beloved by a tall, fine-looking young man with a large income and a charming voice. A chivalrous young man. He had fought the good fight with his mother, who considered that honourable intentions were unnecessary when dealing with chorus girls. There the two were – engaged.

Then China had madly jilted this marvel, this paragon, and had secretly married the short, swarthy violinist of a

18

Manchester café. She had spent the rest of the tour getting telegraphic appeals from her husband; 'Please send five pounds at once Antonio,' or something like that. Which entailed putting her wrist watch into various pawnshops and taking it out again. Constantly. 'Well it serves her right, doesn't it?' said all the other girls.

'No money. Nothing at all,' repeated Marya. 'My father and mother are both dead. My aunt . . .'

'I know; you told me,' interrupted Monsieur Zelli, who had long ago asked adroit questions and found out all there was to find out about Marya's relations. He had reflected that they didn't seem to care in the least what became of her and that English ideas of family life were sometimes exceedingly strange. But he had made no remark.

'It's a pity,' said Monsieur Zelli. 'It's better when a woman has some money, I think. It's much safer for her.'

'I owe for the dress I have on,' Marya informed him, for she was determined to make things perfectly clear.

He told her that they would go next day and pay for it.

'How much do you owe?'

'It's not worth that,' he remarked calmly when she told him. 'Not that it is ugly, but it has no chic. I expect your dressmaker cheats you.'

Marya was annoyed but impressed.

'You know – you'll be happy with me,' he continued in a persuasive voice.

And Marya answered that she dared say she would.

On a June afternoon, heavy with heat, they arrived in Paris.

*

Stephan had lived in Montmartre for fifteen years, he told her, but he had no intimate friends and very few acquaintances. Sometimes he took her with him to some obscure café where he would meet an odd-looking old man or a very smartly-dressed young one. She would sit in the musty-smelling half-light sipping iced beer and listening to long, rapid jabberings: 'La Vierge au coussin vert – Première version – Authentique – Documents – Collier de l'Impératrice Eugénie . . .'

'An amethyst necklace, the stones as big as a calf's eye and set in gold. The pendant pear-shaped, the size of a pigeon's egg. The necklace is strung on a fine gold chain and set with pearls of an extraordinary purity.' The whole to be hung as quickly as possible round the neck of Mrs Buckell A. Butcher of something-or-the-other, Pa, or of any lady willing to put up with an old-fashioned piece of jewellery, because impératrice is a fine word and even empress isn't so bad.

Stephan seemed to do most of his business in cafés. He explained that he acted as intermediary between Frenchmen who wished to sell and foreigners (invariably foreigners) who wished to buy pictures, fur coats, twelfth-century Madonnas, Madame du Barry's prie-Dieu, anything.

Once he had sold a rocking-horse played with by one of Millet's many children, and that had been a very profitable deal indeed.

One evening she had come home to find Napoleon's sabre lying naked and astonishing on her bed by the side of its cedar-wood case.

('Oui, parfaitement,' said Stephan. 'Napoleon's sabre.')

One of his sabres, she supposed. He must have had several of them, of course. A man like Napoleon. Lots. She walked round to the other side of the bed and stared at it, feeling vaguely uneasy. There was a long description of the treasure on the cedar-wood case.

'There are two sheaths, the first of porcelain inlaid with gold, the second of gold set with precious stones. The hilt of the sabre is in gold worked in the Oriental fashion. The blade is of the finest Damascus steel and on it is engraved: "In token of submission, respect and esteem to Napoleon Bonaparte, the hero of Aboukir – Mouhrad Bey".'

That night, long after the cedar-wood case had been packed away in a shabby valise, Marya lay awake thinking.

'Stephan,' she said at last.

'Well?' answered Stephan. He was smoking in front of the open window. 'I thought you were asleep.'

'No,' said Marya. 'Wherever did you get that thing?'

He explained that it belonged to an old French family.

'They're very poor now and they want to sell it. That's all. Why don't they what? The man has to do it on the sly because his mother and his uncle would stop him if they could.'

Marya sat up in bed, put her arms round her knees and said in an unhappy voice:

'He probably has no right to sell it without his mother's consent.'

'His mother has nothing to say,' remarked Stephan sharply. 'But she would bother him if she could.'

Next morning he went out very early, carrying the old valise, and Marya never knew what became of the sabre.

'America,' said Stephan vaguely when she asked. As who should say 'The sea.'

He never explained his doings. He was a secretive person,

she considered. Sometimes, without warning or explanation, he would go away for two or three days, and, left alone in the hotel, she dreaded, not desertion, but some vague, dimly-apprehended catastrophe. But nothing happened. It was a fantastic life, but it kept on its legs so to speak. There was no catastrophe. And eventually Marya stopped questioning and was happy.

Stephan was secretive and a liar, but he was a very gentle and expert lover. She was the petted, cherished child, the desired mistress, the worshipped, perfumed goddess. She was all these things to Stephan – or so he made her believe. Marya hadn't known that a man could be as nice as all that to a woman – so gentle in little ways.

And, besides, she liked him. She liked his wild gaieties and his sudden, obstinate silences and the way he sometimes stretched his hands out to her. Groping. Like a little boy, she would think.

Eighteen months later they went to Brussels for a year. By the time they returned to Paris every vestige of suspicion had left her. She felt that her marriage, though risky, had been a success. And that was that. Her life swayed regularly, even monotonously, between two extremes, avoiding the soul-destroying middle. Sometimes they had a good deal of money and immediately spent it. Sometimes they had almost none at all and then they would skip a meal and drink iced white wine on their balcony instead.

From the balcony Marya could see one side of the Place Blanche. Opposite, the Rue Lepic mounted upwards to the rustic heights of Montmartre. It was astonishing how significant, coherent and understandable it all became after a glass of wine on an empty stomach.

The lights winking up at a pallid moon, the slender painted ladies, the wings of the Moulin Rouge, the smell of petrol and perfume and cooking.

The Place Blanche, Paris, Life itself. One realized all sorts of things. The value of an illusion, for instance, and that the shadow can be more important than the substance. All sorts of things.

3

'GOOD EVENING, Madame Zelli,' said the *patronne* of the Hôtel de l'Univers. 'Will you come in here for a moment? I have something to say to you. Edouard, give the lady a chair.'

There was a small sitting-room behind the hotel bureau where Madame Hautchamp and her husband spent more than half their lives, quite happily so far as one could see. It was a dim, airless place crammed with furniture: a large table, a small table, three straight-backed chairs.

Monsieur Hautchamp, a hairy little man with vague and kindly eyes, muttered something and withdrew.

'Of course,' decided Marya, 'they are going to raise the rent.' She waited.

Madame Hautchamp, who was a large, aquiline lady with a detached and inscrutable expression, announced:

'Your husband will not return tonight, Madame.'

'Oh!' said Marya. 'Ah! *Bon!* Did he telephone?'

She looked at a loudly-ticking clock on the mantelshelf. It was just eight.

'Monsieur,' said the *patronne*, 'has been arrested. Yes, Madame, arrested. About an hour ago, about seven o'clock. An inspector and an agent came here. *Enfin . . .*'

She gesticulated with both hands and one eyebrow.

'I understand nothing of all this, nothing. Unhappily, there is no doubt at all that he has been arrested.'

24

Silence.

Then Marya asked in a careful voice: 'He didn't — say anything before he went?'

'Monsieur asked, I think, if he could leave a letter for you, and the inspector refused.'

'Oh, did he?' said Marya, staring at Madame Hautchamp.

Her heart had stopped; then began to beat so violently that she felt sick. Her hands were damp and cold. Something in her brain was shrieking triumphantly: 'There you are! I knew it! I told you so!'

The *patronne* remarked, after another pause: 'These things are disagreeable, very disagreeable for everybody. Nobody likes to be mixed up with these things.'

The inflection of her voice aroused in Marya some useful instinct of self-defence, and she was able to say that it was evidently a mistake.

'Oh, evidently,' agreed Madame Hautchamp politely. She looked at her client with curiosity and added: 'Well, don't torment yourself too much. The police! Why, the police arrest people for nothing at all! It's perfectly ridiculous. They have some idea — I don't know — they say that there is a bolshevist plot in Paris. They arrest this one, that one. Meanwhile the *voyous* go free. In your place, I should wait for news without tormenting myself, Madame.'

As Marya climbed the stairs to her room her legs were trembling. She was obliged to hold on to the banisters.

'I must go and find De Solla,' she told herself. Her mind clung desperately to the thought of Miss De Solla's calm, her deep and masculine voice.

*

It was raining and the lights of the Moulin Rouge shone redly through a mist: Salle de danse, Revue.

The Grelot was illuminated. The Place Blanche, sometimes so innocently sleepy of an afternoon, was getting ready for the night's work. People hurried along cowering beneath their umbrellas, and the pavements were slippery and glistening, with pools of water here and there, sad little mirrors which the reflections of the lights tinted with a dull point of red. The trees along the Boulevard Clichy stretched ridiculously frail and naked arms to a sky without stars.

Marya emerged from the Métro on to the Place Denfert-Rochereau, thinking: 'In three minutes I'll hear somebody talking English. In two minutes, in a minute.' She ran along the Avénue d'Orléans. But Miss De Solla's studio was in darkness. She knocked, and a woman put her head out of a door on the other side of the courtyard and said that Mademoiselle had gone to London. Mademoiselle might be away for some weeks, but a letter would be forwarded.

'Ah, I didn't know she'd gone,' said Marya.

She stood staring at the dark windows for a minute, then walked very slowly away. As she turned the corner of the Rue Denfert-Rochereau she saw the Heidlers on the other side of the street. They were walking against the wind, both sheltering under a huge umbrella. A gust of wind flapped Heidler's mackintosh like a flag, caught the umbrella and blew it sideways. She saw his annoyed face.

She thought: 'What's it got to do with them, anyway, and what can they do?' She went along up the street. People turned and stared at her because she was walking so slowly in the pouring rain.

*

She spent several hours of the following day in the annexe of the Palais de Justice on the Quai des Orfèvres. Every half-hour she consulted a tall, fat-faced man in a black robe who, she had been told, would be able to tell her why her husband had been arrested.

'What name?' the fat-faced man would ask wearily.

When she told him, he would run his finger down a list and say: 'No information.'

Then a lesser light would enter with a pile of fresh documents, and Marya would go back to her bench and wait. The bench was of an incredible hardness – the room was big and draughty – her back hurt.

On one side of her sat a very respectable lady dressed in black who had brought her *bonne* with her. The companion was evidently a *bonne*, for she wore the Breton cap and apron, and, in spite of the whiteness of the linen, she looked very dirty. They both looked dirty, and they whispered interminably ssp . . . ssp . . . ssp.

On the other side sat a young man with new shoes of a bright reddish yellow, his coat and trousers were tight, his hat very small, no overcoat. He seemed gay and carefree, and whistled a little tune as he looked with childish and affectionate pride at his shoes, and then with sympathy at Marya. He asked at last how long she had been there, and when she told him: 'Oh, they don't hurry themselves, *ces messieurs*. We'll take root here in the end,' he prophesied cheerfully.

Everyone else sat as mournfully still as though they were part of the sombre décor of some incredibly dull play. Sometimes a dapper gentleman with an official air would walk quickly through the outer room and smartly into the inner one and then reappear after an interval looking subdued.

Five o'clock.

'What name?' asked the fat-faced man for the sixth time. 'But I tell you I have no information. No, none. I won't know today – it's too late. You'd better go to the Palais de Justice tomorrow morning.'

'Oh, but I must know now,' Marya told him. 'I must know. It's my husband.'

'If it's your husband or your brother, or your father or your uncle, it's just the same,' said the fat-faced man. 'I don't know.'

He added very indignantly: 'No! But!'

The warder who had directed her to the office of the fat-faced man asked, as she passed him, if she had the information she wanted. She shook her head and began to cry. Her back hurt. She was too tired to be able to bear a kind voice.

'*Ah, là, là,*' said the warder. 'But it's probably nothing. Nothing at all. Reckless driving. Three days. Come, come. Nothing to cry about, *ma petite dame*. Courage!'

A colleague asked him what he knew about the matter and he turned to explain:

'I can't see a woman cry. When I see a woman cry, I am forced to try to comfort her. *C'est plus fort que moi.*'

He began again earnestly: '*Ma petite dame . . .*'

Marya had already walked on.

'Not that way out,' said a vague voice.

She faced round, passed under an archway, and was on the peaceful Quai des Orfèvres. She stayed there for a long time watching the trembling reflections of the lights on the

28

Seine. Yellow lights like jewels, like eyes that winked at her. Red lights like splashes of blood on the stealthy water. Necklaces of lights over the dark, slowly moving water.

She stayed there till a passing youth called: 'Hé, little one. Is it for tonight the suicide?'

Then she hailed a taxi and went back to Montmartre, thinking indifferently as she paid the driver: 'And I haven't much money, either. This is a beautiful muddle I'm in.'

*

Next day she went to the Palais de Justice.

Shining gates, ascending flights of steps. *Liberté*, *Egalité*, *Fraternité* in golden letters; *Tribunal de Police* in black. As it were, a vision of heaven and the Judgment.

She was hurrying along corridors and up staircases after a bright little man in horn-rimmed spectacles, who had informed her that he was a journalist and asked if he could be of any service to her. He knew the Palais very well indeed, he said. He would dart at a door, tap on it, ask a rapid question and set off again in the opposite direction, and Marya, hastening after him, began to feel as though she were playing some intricate game of which she did not understand the rules. As they ran he talked about the bolshevist scare. He said that the arrests had become a scandal, that it was time that they were stopped, that they would be stopped.

'That's what we are here for, we others, we journalists.' Every time she thanked him breathlessly, he would answer: 'I am only too happy to assist a confrère.'

She wondered why he imagined that Stephan was a

journalist. 'Now what have I said to make him think that?' she worried.

He rapped at a final door. Two gentlemen wearing long black robes, little white collars and full black beards, looked at them with inquiry.

'The husband of Madame,' explained Marya's friend, 'a Monsieur Stephan Zelli, a confrère,' he smiled and bowed again, 'has been arrested. She is naturally anxious, very anxious indeed to know the reason of his arrest.'

Fluent explanations flowed gently and persuasively from him. Clever little man! And he was going to get what he wanted, too, for one of the lawyers got up, looked through a pile of documents and came back with a dossier. He said:

'Zelli, Stephan. Aha! You wish to know the cause of the arrest? It is an affair of theft, of *escroquerie*.'

The journalist cleared his throat and coughed.

'*Bon soir, Madame, bon soir*,' he said hurriedly. 'I'm most happy to have been of service to you.' He backed towards the door, looking nervous as though he were afraid she would try to keep him with her, drag him by force into her disreputable existence. '*Bon soir, bon soir!*' he kept saying in a bright voice. And vanished.

'Is it a very serious affair?' asked Marya.

She thought of all the corridors and staircases which had led her to this dim, musty-smelling room and felt bewildered and giddy.

Both the lawyers laughed heartily and one of them threw his head back to do it, opening his mouth widely and showing a long pink and white tongue and the beginnings of a palate.

'Theft, Madame,' he said reproachfully, when he had

finished laughing, 'is always a serious affair.' He ran hard eyes over her with the look of an expert passing intimate judgments, smiled again and asked her nationality. 'Polish, also?'

'No,' said Marya. She got up.

The less flippant gentleman with the longer beard said that that was all they could tell her.

'Your husband has been arrested on a charge – several charges – of theft. He is in the Prison de la Santé and you will probably hear from him in a day or two. You can get a permit to see him in the annexe, Quai des Orfèvres.'

'Thank you,' said Marya.

4

A LETTER FROM Stephan arrived next morning.

My dear Mado,

I fear that you must be most unquiet. Still I could not write for the reason that I was not allowed to up till yet. When I came in that evening I found two men waiting for me and they showed me the warrant for my arrest. I am accused of selling stolen pictures and other things. This is ridiculous. However, here I am, and I don't think that they will let me go as quickly as all that. Except I can find a very good lawyer. Everything will depend on my lawyer. Come to see me on Thursday, the day of the visits, and I will try to explain things. My dear, I have such a cafard.

Stephan

'It's a pity all the same,' thought the watching Madame Hautchamp, who noticed that the young woman was pale and had a troublesome cough. 'Ah, all these people,' she thought.

Madame Hautchamp meant all of them. All the strange couples who filled her hotel – internationalists who invariably got into trouble sooner or later. She went back into the sitting-room and remarked as much to Monsieur Hautchamp, who was reading the newspaper, and Monsieur Hautchamp shrugged his shoulders; then, with an expression of profound disapproval, he continued his article which, as it happened, began thus:

'*Le mélange des races est à la base de l'èvolution humaine vers le type parfait.*'

'I don't think,' thought Monsieur Hautchamp – or something to that effect.

Marya folded her letter, which was written in English on cheap, blue-lined paper, put it carefully into her handbag, and walked out into the Place Blanche. She spent the foggy day in endless, aimless walking, for it seemed to her that if she moved quickly enough she would escape the fear that hunted her. It was a vague and shadowy fear of something cruel and stupid that had caught her and would never let her go. She had always known that it was there – hidden under the more or less pleasant surface of things. Always. Ever since she was a child.

You could argue about hunger or cold or loneliness, but with that fear you couldn't argue. It went too deep. You were too mysteriously sure of its terror. You could only walk very fast and try to leave it behind you.

That evening she sat for a long while in a small bar drinking coffee and after the third glass composed a letter to England asking for some money. Then: 'But they haven't got any to send,' she thought. 'I won't tell them yet anyhow. What's the use?'

She tore the letter up. She told herself: 'I've got to be sensible. I'll get out of this all right if I'm sensible. I've got to have some guts, as Albert Prance would say.'

Opposite her a pale, long-faced girl sat in front of an untouched drink, watching the door. She was waiting for the gentleman with whom she had spent the preceding night to come along and pay for it, and naturally she was waiting in vain. Her mouth drooped, her eyes were desolate and humble.

*

Marya went back to her bedroom from the misty streets and shut the door with a feeling of relief as if she had shut out a malignant world. Her bedroom was a refuge. She undressed slowly, thinking: 'Funny this room is without Stephan.' Empty it looked and full of shadows. Every now and again she would stop undressing and listen, half expecting to hear him coming along the passage.

When she lay down she put out her hand and touched his pillow gently. . . . Stephan. He was a bad lot. Possibly. Well, obviously. And what if he were? 'I don't care,' thought Marya. 'He's been kind to me. We've been friends. We've had fun together. I don't care what he is.'

She turned several times uneasily; then sighed, put on the light and lit a cigarette with shaking hands. Humbug it all was. The rotten things that people did. The mean things they got away with – sailed away with – smirking. Nobody caring a bit. Didn't she know something about that? Didn't she, though! But, of course, anything to do with money was swooped on and punished ferociously.

'Humbug!' she said aloud.

But as soon as she put the light out the fear was with her again – and now it was like a long street where she walked endlessly. A redly lit street, the houses on either side tall, grey and closely shuttered, the only sound the clip-clop of horses' hoofs behind her, out of sight.

In the morning she went back to the Quai des Orfèvres and was given a permit to visit the Santé prison. Marya Zelli, aged 28 years, British by birth. Polish by marriage. . . . And so on, and so on.

*

The outside wall of the Santé frowns down on the Boulevard Arago. Three hundred blackened yards of it, sombre and hopeless. Also it seemed never-ending and there was no sign of an entrance. Eventually Marya asked a policeman who was pacing up and down outside to direct her, and when he stared, she told him in a low voice that she wished to visit one of the prisoners. He jerked a thumb over his shoulder in the direction of a side-street and turned his back. Inside the entrance a fat, blond warder with a pear-shaped stomach, who sat overlapping a very small chair, waved her onwards with an austere and majestic gesture. She crossed a courtyard paved with grey cobblestones and ascended a flight of stairs into an entrance hall where a bevy of warders were waiting fussily to take the permits. 'It's rather like giving up one's ticket in a Paris theatre,' thought Marya.

She went into the *parloir*, which was a huge room full of the buzz of voices. One of the warders opened the door of a small cubicle, and she sat down on a wooden bench and stared steadily through bars that were like bars of an animal's cage. Her heart began to beat heavily. The buzzing noise deafened and benumbed her. She felt as though an iron band were encircling her head tightly, as though she were sinking slowly down into deep water.

Stephan appeared on the other side suddenly, as if he had somehow been shot out of a trap.

'Hallo, Mado!'

'Hallo,' she said. 'My poor boy, what rotten luck!'

'I think,' said Stephan, glancing round nervously, 'that we are supposed to talk French. Can you hear what I say?' he asked.

'Of course.'

'Well, this hellish noise. One would say that the whole of Paris is in here, yelling. Mado, listen, the worst, the very worst is that this has happened when I have no money. You must write to England at once for money. Have you written yet?'

She answered cautiously: 'Well, I've written, but they haven't much to send, you know. What's the use of worrying them when they can't really help? But I'll be all right,' she added fretfully; 'I'll manage something for myself. Of course, there must be heaps of things I can do, only I've got an awful cold and I can't think properly.'

She felt awkward and ill at ease. It was horrible to see his face peering at her through bars, thin and furtive, scarcely like Stephan at all. She said:

'Tell me what happened exactly. I would rather know.'

He moved his head from side to side awkwardly.

'Well, I told you in my letter, didn't I?'

He doesn't want to tell me, she thought. And, after all, what does it matter? The iron band round her head was drawn tighter.

He began to talk rapidly, gesticulating, but what he said conveyed nothing at all to her. She had suddenly ceased to be able to understand French. He had become strangely remote.

'And not a sou on me when I was arrested,' continued Stephan. 'That's the stupid thing. That it should have happened just now.' He swore softly: '*Nom de Dieu*! It's you I am worrying about.'

'Oh, I'll be all right,' said Marya.

The warder banged the door open. They grimaced smiles at each other.

At the beginning of the next week she sold her dresses. She lay in bed, for her cold had become feverish. The garments were spread over a chair ready for the inspection of Madame Hautchamp, who, sympathetic without for one moment allowing her sympathy to overflow a certain limit of business-like correctness, explained:

'My sister-in-law is a *teinturière* and I can make an arrangement with her to hang them for sale in her window, otherwise I could not buy them at all. And, as it is, I can't offer you very much. This, for instance, this *robe de soirée* . . .' She pointed out the gem of the collection: 'Who would buy it? Nobody. Except a woman *qui fait la noce*. Fortunately, my sister-in-law has several clients *qui font la noce*.'

'But I don't see why it must be that sort of woman,' argued Marya.

'It's not a practical dress,' said Madame Hautchamp calmly; 'it's a fantasy, one may say. Therefore, if it is bought at all, it will be bought by that kind of woman. Fortunately, as I have told you, my sister-in-law has several clients . . .'

Madame Hautchamp was formidable. One heard the wheels of society clanking as she spoke. No mixing. No

37

ill feeling either. All so inevitable that one could only bow the head and submit.

'I can give you two hundred and fifty francs,' calculated Madame Hautchamp, looking like a well coiffured eagle with a gift for bargaining.

'All right,' said Marya. She shivered, shut her eyes, moved her head uneasily to find a cool place on the pillow.

'Ah, how stupid I am!' said the lady, gathering up the dresses. 'This pneumatique came for you.'

'Dear Madame Zelli,' wrote Mrs Heidler. 'We had your address from Miss De Solla. Would you care to dine with us tomorrow night and go on to a party given by an American friend of ours whom I'm sure you'll like? Lefranc's at half-past eight. I do hope you will be able to come.'

5

'WELL,' SAID HEIDLER, 'here's hoping.'

Marya smiled and answered: 'Here's hoping.'

She was cold. Her feet were soaked. She imagined that all the people in the restaurant looked sleek, tidy and placid, and envied their well-ordered lives. Then the vermouth warmed her throat and chest and she felt less physically miserable.

'Monsieur Lefranc,' called Heidler.

The patron hurried up to the table; a quick, lively little man, but sparing of word and gesture, recommending this or that with an air as if to say: 'And I wouldn't do this for everybody, mind you.' One saw at once why English people patronized his restaurant. That decent restraint gave them confidence.

Mrs Heidler observed her guest with calm brown eyes.

'But you're wet through, poor child!'

Marya answered that it was nothing, just the sleeve of her coat.

'Then take it off,' advised Mrs Heidler.

She looked past Marya at a girl dressed in red, followed by two young men, who passed the table with coldly averted head.

'Well,' she said, 'did you see Cri-Cri cut me dead, H. J.? Considering that she came to my party last Saturday.'

Cri-Cri, who was a bold spirit and a good sort, sat down

with her legs widely apart like some hardy cavalier, seized the menu and began to talk rapidly in a rather cantankerous voice. She was a small, plump girl with an astonishingly accurate make-up, a make-up which never varied, day in and day out, week in and week out. Her round cheeks were painted orange-red, her lips vermilion, her green eyes shadowed with kohl, her pointed nose dead white. There was never too much or too little, or a lock of her sleek black hair out of place. A wonderful performance. She was the famous model of a Japanese painter, also a cabaret singer and a character; and she had ignored the Heidlers because she realized that she could afford to display coldness, and that no good ever comes from being too polite.

Mrs Heidler watched her with a wistful expression, for she was unable to avoid putting a fictitious value on anyone who snubbed her, and she was really anxious to have people like Cri-Cri at her parties. People who got written about. Characters. Types. She began to discuss the famous lady, characters in general, beauty.

'It's an angle of the eyes and mouth,' said Mrs Heidler. She repeated, satisfied: 'That's what it is. I've noticed it over and over again. It's a certain angle of the eyes and mouth.'

Monsieur Lefranc served the fish.

When Marya looked across the table at Heidler, she noticed that he had oddly shaped eyelids, three cornered eyelids over pale, clever eyes. Not at all an amiable looking person. But nevertheless not without understanding, for every time that her glass was empty he refilled it. She began to feel miraculously reassured, happy and secure. Her thoughts were vague and pleasant, her misery distant as the sound of the rain. She watched through a slight mist a party of people who had just come into the restaurant, the movements of arms taking off overcoats, of legs in light-coloured stockings and feet in low-heeled shoes walking over the wooden floor to hide themselves under the table-cloths. Against a blurred background she saw, with enormous distinctness, a woman's profile, another's back, the row of bottles on the counter, a man's shoulders and his striped tie. Marya sat very upright on the leather bench, talking carefully and coherently. A confused murmur of voices – Mrs Heidler's loud and authoritative, Heidler's gentle and hesitating.

'Oh, Lola,' Heidler was saying, 'Lola is Elizabethan.' They were still discussing types.

The grey-blue room seemed to be growing larger, the walls had receded, the bulbs of the electric lights had expanded mysteriously. Now they looked like small moons.

'Ah, there you are, Anna,' said Mrs Heidler to a small, neat American, with baby-blonde hair, a keen eye and a very firm mouth indeed.

'Lola is in the Select,' remarked this lady. 'She'll be along in a minute.'

Miss Lola Hewitt arrived, accompanied by a fresh-faced youth who wore a *béret basque*, a jersey, and very shabby trousers. Lola was a pretty lady, but she seemed moody. Her long thin fingers twitched on the stem of her glass, and she announced: 'Oh, I am not in my *assiette*, as the dear French say.'

'Darling,' Lois told her, 'don't get depressed. Have another *fine*.'

A gaunt lady wearing a turban was also, it seemed, going

41

to the party; so was a pleasant gentleman who sat down next to Marya and invited her to meet him in the Dôme at half-past ten on the following morning. He added cheerfully: 'I didn't catch your name. Mine's Porson.' And Marya realized from his tone that Mr Porson must be a celebrated person. The turbaned lady was saying jerkily: 'It's a pity about Rolls and the literary gathering, isn't it? Yes, he's got a literary gathering on this evening at the Café Lavenue. Nine o'clock. Rolls and Boyes. Both of them. All the Middle Westerners are going.'

'I say,' persisted Porson, 'couldn't you turn up to-morrow? I wish you would. I feel that I'd like to talk to you. I know that half-past ten is a bit early, but I'm going back to London in the afternoon.' He added, drooping his head mournfully, that he had been getting divorced. 'And it's a miserable business. Oh, wretched! Most depressing.'

It was difficult to listen to the details of Mr Porson's divorce. Marya heard the fresh-faced boy saying: 'I can drink whatever I like, and pull myself together in a minute with the stuff.'

'What is it?' she said, leaning over to him. 'Let me look.'

'Would you like to try one?' asked the boy. He handed her over a small capsule. 'Break it, sniff it up, that's right.'

Marya broke the capsule and inhaled. Her heart stopped with a jerk, then seemed to dilate suddenly and very painfully. The blood rushed over her face and neck. 'I'm going to fall,' she thought with terror, and clutched the edge of the table.

'That got you all right,' said the fresh-faced boy, interested. He appealed to the others: 'I say, do look. She got that all right, didn't she?'

From a great distance Marya heard the voice of the lady with the turban: 'Rolls is, of course, the great stylist, but Boyes – Boyes is the pioneer.'

'I'm so sorry,' she began. Then she explained, speaking carefully, that she was afraid she could not go on to the party, that she was afraid that she must go straight home. 'I've had flu and it's pulled me down a bit. I must go home,' she muttered, looking at Heidler with appeal.

'Of course,' he said. 'It's still pouring; you must have a taxi.'

As they walked to the door she felt passionately grateful to him. She was sure that he knew she was ill and near to tears. He was a rock of a man with his big shoulders and his quiet voice.

'Good night,' he said. 'Lois will look you up as soon as we get back from Brunoy. Take care of that cough. Don't worry.'

He shut the taxi door.

6

TEN DAYS LATER Stephan was tried and sentenced to a
year's imprisonment to be followed by expulsion from
France. Marya went to the Santé to see him, feeling
exhausted, listless, drained of all capacity for emotion.
But as soon as she entered the dark courtyard of the prison
her indifference vanished. In the *parloir* a warder opened
the door of a cubicle and signed to her. She waited, breathless, trembling a little.

When Stephan appeared: 'I've been ill,' she began, 'or
I'd have come to the Palais de Justice for your trial.'

'But I asked you not to,' answered Stephan. 'Didn't you
get my letter? Well . . . no luck.'

He was unshaven and collarless. He sat huddled up on
the wooden seat, staring at her with sunken, reddened
eyes. 'I'm not going to be able to stand it,' he said in a
small voice – a little boy's voice. 'I can't. I can't.'

The loud conversations from the neighbouring cubicles
were like the buzzing of gigantic insects. Inexorable, be-
wildering noise.

'I have such a cafard when I think of you, Mado.'

Marya said: 'Well, I expect I'll be all right. The
Heidlers.' She pressed her hands tightly together in her
lap. 'I mustn't cry, whatever I do,' she was thinking.

'Heidlers?' questioned Stephen vaguely.

'Mrs Heidler came to see me just after I got your letter

and I told her. I'm sorry. I didn't mean to give you away; but I felt, you know – awful.'

'Oh, what's it matter?' said Stephan. '*Je m'en fiche.*' Then he added, curiously: 'What did she say?'

'Nothing very much. I think she's a good sort.' She stopped, remembering Lois's voice when she remarked: 'Of course, something's got to be done about it, my dear.' A masterful voice.

'I'm going to see them tonight,' she went on. 'They will probably be able to help me to a job or something. Besides, I can get a little money from England. I'll be all right.'

They sat in silence for a time, then he told her that he was going to be sent to Fresnes, not to a central prison.

'Fresnes is quite near Paris. Will you come and see me?'

'Of course, of course. . . . Stephan, listen. Don't worry, my dear. You'll be free in September, won't you? It isn't so long. The time will pass quickly.' Not very clever that. But her brain wasn't working properly.

'Quickly! My God, that's funny! Quickly!'

He laughed, but she thought that he looked as though he were begging for help, and she felt desperate with the longing to comfort him.

'I love you,' she said.

'*C'est vrai?*' asked Stephan. 'Well, perhaps. I'll see that.'

She repeated: 'I love you. Don't be too sad, my dear.' But hopelessly, for she felt that he was withdrawn from her, enclosed in the circle of his own pain, unreachable.

A warder behind him flung the door open and he jumped

up with an alacrity which she thought dreadful, shocking.

'So long!' he said in English, smiling his grimace of a smile.

The warder bawled something. He started like a nervous horse and disappeared from her view.

*

It was a foggy afternoon, with a cold sharpness in the air. Outside, the street lamps were lit. 'It might be London,' thought Marya. The Boulevard Arago, like everything else, seemed unreal, fantastic, but also extraordinarily familiar, and she was trying to account for this mysterious impression of familiarity.

She felt cold when she reached the Avenue d'Orléans and walked into a bar for some hot coffee. The place was empty save for a big man who was sitting opposite drinking a demi of dark beer. He stared at Marya steadily and heavily as he drank, and when she took Stephan's letter out of her bag and reread it he thought: 'Doubtless a rendezvous.'

'My lawyer didn't know his métier. Instead of defending me he told the court that I knew six languages. A stupid affair at Brussels was referred to. This did me in quite . . .'

A stupid affair at Brussels. But when she tried to think this out her tired brain would only conjure up disconnected remembrances of Brussels: waiters in white jackets bearing aloft tall, slim glasses of beer, the Paris train clanking into the dark station, the sun on the red-striped umbrellas in the flower market, the green trees of the Avenue Louise.

She sat there, smoking cigarette after cigarette, long after the large man had disappeared. Every time that the door of the café swung open to admit a customer she saw the crimson lights of the tobacco shop opposite and the crimson reflection on the asphalt and she began to picture the endless labyrinth of the Paris streets, glistening hardly, crowded with hurrying people. But now she thought of them without fear, rather with a strange excitement.

'What's the use of worrying about things?' she asked herself. 'I don't care. I'm sick of being sad.'

She came out of the café and stood for several minutes looking at the Lion de Belfort fair – the booths, the swings, the crowds of people jostling each other in a white glare of light to the gay, metallic music of the merry-go-rounds.

*

The Heidlers were waiting at August's Restaurant on the Boulevard St Michel. At a quarter to nine Heidler said:

'I hope nothing's happened to that girl.'

And as Lois was answering that she thought not, she hoped not, Marya entered the restaurant. She was very pale, her eyes were shadowed, her lips hastily and inadequately rouged. She was wearing a black dress under her coat, a sleeveless, shapeless, sack-like garment, and she appeared frail, childish, and extraordinarily shabby.

'Shall I tell her, H. J.?' asked Lois.

'Why not?' answered Heidler, looking majestic but slightly embarrassed.

'Don't look frightened,' said Lois.

Marya glanced rapidly from one to the other and repeated, 'Frightened—?'

'It's something that you'll like, or at any rate I hope

47

you will. You know, H. J. and I have been thinking a lot about you. And, my dear, you can't be left alone like this. I mean, it's impossible, isn't it?'

She put out her hand caressingly. Marya thought how odd it was that she could never make up her mind whether she liked or intensely disliked Mrs Heidler's touch.

Lois went on: 'Now, look here, we want you to move into the spare room at the studio.' Because she was nervous her voice was even more authoritative than usual. 'It's only a cubby-hole of a place, but you'll be all right there. And you must stay till you've made up your mind what you're going to do. Till you're better. As long as you like, my dear.'

Silence.

Monsieur August placed a large sole on the table, glanced at Heidler with light blue, very ironical eyes, and departed.

'Imposing looking chap, August,' remarked Heidler. He fidgeted. He seemed shy.

Marya said in a low voice: 'I don't know how to thank you. It's so awfully good of you to worry about me. . . .'

Heidler remarked with an air of relief that as it was all decided they needn't talk about it any more. Marya smiled a difficult smile. She told herself: 'These people are wonderfully kind, but I certainly don't want to go and live with them. And so I shan't go. There's nothing to worry about.'

'When can you move?' asked Heidler. 'Tomorrow?'

'But,' said Marya, 'I'm afraid I shall be an awful bother.'

'That's all right!' Heidler assured her. His eyes met hers for a second, then he looked quickly away.

'I'm really afraid,' she persisted, 'that it's quite impossible. You're wonderfully kind, but I couldn't dream of bothering you.'

'Rubbish!' said Lois. 'We'd love to have you and it's all arranged. After dinner you must come round to the studio and we'll talk things over. H. J.'s got to go over the other side to see somebody.'

Marya agreed with relief. 'Yes, we'll talk things over.' She was silent and subdued for the rest of the meal.

When Lois announced: 'I shall certainly want to paint you. In that black dress, I think, and short black gloves. Or shall I have short green gloves? What d'you think, H. J.?' she began to wonder why the idea of living with the Heidlers filled her with such extraordinary dismay. After all, she told herself, it might be fun.

*

The two women walked along the Boulevard St Michel behind their distorted shadows. They walked in silence, close together, almost touching each other, and as they walked Lois was thinking: 'She can't make her mouth up. The poor little devil has got no harm in her and I shouldn't mind doing her a good turn. She won't be much trouble.'

They passed the deserted entrance of the Bal Bullier and the coloured lights of the Closerie des Lilas, and crossed the street into the dimness of the Avenue de l'Observatoire, where the tops of the trees vanished, ghost-like, in the mist.

The Heidlers lived on the second floor of a high building half-way up the street. The outer door was shut, and, as they waited, Lois began to talk about the concierge. She told Marya that they had a beast of a concierge.

'At one of my Saturday parties,' she explained, 'Swansee Grettle— D'you know her? She's a fine gel. She sculpts. Well, Swansee complained that one of the men had kicked her on purpose. So Swansee's man took the other man out on the landing and fought him.'

The door flew open, and Mrs Heidler led the way up the wooden, uncarpeted staircase, still talking.

'Well, Swansee's man got a bang on the nose and bled all over the place, and when the concierge saw what she had to mop up next morning she made a dreadful row and has been vile to us ever since. Of course, this place is only a makeshift really till we can find something better. Come in here.'

The studio was a big, high-ceilinged room, sparsely furnished, dimly lit. A doll dressed as an eighteenth-century lady smirked conceitedly on the divan, with satin skirts spread stiffly. There was an elaborate gramophone, several cards were stuck into the looking-glass over the mantelpiece. There was a portrait on the wall above the looking-glass, carefully painted but smug and slightly pretentious, like a coloured photograph. Marya thought: 'It's perfectly extraordinary that Heidler should live in a room like this.'

'I'll go and get some cigarettes for you,' Lois told her. 'Lie down on the divan. You look tired.'

She said when she came back: 'You don't want to come and stay with us, do you? Now, why? What's the fuss about? If you really mean that you're afraid of being a bother, put that right out of your head. I'm used to it.

H. J.'s always rescuing some young genius or the other and installing him in the spare bedroom... Many's the one we've pulled out of a hole since we've been in Montparnesse, I can tell you.' She added: 'And they invariably hate us bitterly afterwards. Never mind! Perhaps you'll be the brilliant exception.'

Marya answered vaguely: 'Yes, but it's not a question with me of just tiding over a few days or a few weeks. I really haven't got any money at all and I do feel I ought to do something about it.'

'Well,' said Lois, 'what will you do?' She looked at Marya with a dubious but intelligent expression as if to say: 'Go on. Explain yourself. I'm listening. I'm making an effort to get at your point of view.'

Marya began with difficulty: 'You see, I'm afraid the trouble with me is that I'm not hard enough. I'm a soft, thin-skinned sort of person and I've been frightened to death these last days. I don't at all mean physically frightened . . .' She stopped.

Mrs Heidler still gazed at her with sensible and inquiring brown eyes.

'I've realized, you see, that life is cruel and horrible to unprotected people. I think life is cruel. I think people are cruel.' All the time she spoke she was thinking: 'Why should I tell her all this?' But she felt impelled to go on. 'I may be completely wrong, of course, but that's how I feel. Well, I've got used to the idea of facing cruelty. One can, you know. The moment comes when even the softest person doesn't care a damn any more; and that's a precious moment. One oughtn't to waste it. You're wonderfully kind, but if I come to stay with you it'll only make me soft and timid and I'll have to start getting hard all over again afterwards. I don't suppose,' she added hopelessly, 'that you understand what I mean a bit.'

Lois argued: 'I don't see why you should have to start getting hard all over again afterwards. People aren't such ogres as all that. People can be quite kind if you don't rub them up the wrong way.'

'Can they?' said Marya.

Lois coughed: 'That's all very well, but, getting down to brass tacks, what exactly do you think of doing? I feel a certain responsibility for you. I don't see why I should. I suppose you're the sort of person one does feel responsible for. You were on the stage, weren't you? Well, I hope you're not thinking of trying for a job as a *femme nue* in a music-hall. They don't get paid anything at all, poor dears.'

'I know they don't,' answered Marya. 'No, I won't try to be a *femme nue*. I don't know what I shall do. . . . I don't care, and that's a big advantage, anyway.'

She leaned her head back against the cushions and half shut her eyes. Suddenly she felt horribly tired, giddy with fatigue.

'Of course,' Lois remarked in a reflective voice, 'men . . . a man would possibly . . . yes, in a way . . . But that sort of thing must be done carefully, my girl, or it's the most ghastly fiasco. I mean, even if you make up your mind that it's your best way out, you must plan it very carefully, and however carefully you plan it's often a fiasco, it seems to me.'

'I don't think I'd ever plan anything out carefully,' said Marya, 'and certainly not that. If I went to the devil it would be because I wanted to, or because it's a good drug, or because I don't give a damn for my idiotic body of a woman, anyway. And all the people who yap.' She spoke very quickly, flushed, then burst into tears. 'Now I'm a gone coon,' she thought. 'I've begun to cry and I'll never stop.'

Lois said: 'You see how right I was to tell you that you must come and stay with us, that you mustn't be left alone.' Her voice trembled. Marya was amazed to see tears in her eyes. . . . 'You know,' Lois added, 'H. J., I love him so terribly . . . and he isn't always awfully nice to me.'

They sat side by side on the divan and wept together. Marya wondered how she could ever have thought Lois hard. This soft creature, this fellow-woman, hurt and bewildered by life even as she was. 'She simply is more plucky than I am,' she thought. 'She puts a better face on it.'

Lois was saying: 'When you told me that your husband was in jail – d'you remember? – I felt as if you'd stretched out a hand for help. Well – and I caught hold of your hand. I want to help you. I'll be awfully disappointed and hurt if you don't allow me to.'

'I didn't mean that, really, really,' answered Marya shakily.

Lois blew her nose. Then she remarked with earnestness: 'You mustn't think that I don't see the – the angle you look at life from. Because I do. If I were you I'd hate, loathe, detest everybody safe, everybody with money in the bank.'

'But I wasn't thinking of money so much,' interrupted Marya.

'It's appalling, perfectly appalling,' continued the other

53

in a complacent voice, 'to think of the difference that money makes to a woman's life. I've always said so.'

'Yes, doesn't it?' said Marya.

'Come up and see your room,' Lois suggested, and Marya followed her up a narrow staircase to a little room which smelt clean and cold. Striped grey and green curtains hung straightly over the long windows.

'Now, when do you think you can move?' said Lois briskly. 'Better do it as soon as you can, won't you?'

'You're a darling to worry about me,' answered Marya. 'A darling.'

But as soon as the cold air touched her face outside she felt sobered and melancholy. She hailed a taxi and climbed into it wearily.

'*Ah, ma pauvre vieille!*' she told herself.

7

WHEN THE PARIS tram to Fresnes stopped outside the café called the Cadran Bleu, Marya got down. She walked up a wide road bordered with magnificent trees to the prison, a high, grey building standing in large grounds.

The usual formalities. The usual questioning warders whom she found herself regarding with a mixture of fear and hatred. Then she crossed a cobblestoned courtyard and a dark, dank corridor like the open mouth of a monster swallowed her up. At the extreme end of this corridor a queue of people, mostly women, stood waiting, and as she took her place in the queue she felt a sudden, devastating realization of the essential craziness of existence. She thought again: people are very rum. With all their little arrangements, prisons and drains and things, tucked away where nobody can see.

She waited with cold hands and a beating heart, full of an unreasoning shame at being there at all. Every time the warder approached her she moved her shoulders nervously, and when he laid a fat, lingering hand on the arm of one of the women to push her into place, she thought: if he touches me I shall have to hit him, and then what will happen to me? I'll be locked up, too, as sure as God made Moses.

Eventually she was conducted to the inevitable small, roofless cubicle. A warder paced up and down a wooden platform overhead, stopping every now and again to listen to the conversations. Stephan appeared with a piece of coarse sacking over his head. He was like some bright-eyed animal, staring at her, and she sat in an embarrassed silence, wondering how she could ever have thought that he would be able to talk things over with her or give her advice. At last, spurred by the knowledge that soon the warder would bang on the door and the interview be over, she began to murmur: 'My poor darling, my poor darling, my poor dear.'

'*Oh, ça!*' said Stephan. He shrugged, leaned forward and asked: 'What's that scarf you've got on? I don't know that scarf, do I?'

They talked about the scarf for a time and then she told him that the Heidlers had asked her to go and stay with them.

'Look here, Stephan, I don't want to go a bit,' she added.

'Why not?'

'I don't know.'

'Then, for God's sake, why not?' asked Stephan nervously. 'They're your country-people, aren't they? You understand them and they understand you.'

'I'm not so sure of that,' Marya answered in an obstinate voice.

He went on fretfully:

'Do you want to drive me mad? I wonder if you know what it's like for me shut up here, thinking of you without a sou. Is Mrs Heidler nice?'

'Very nice!'

'A good sort? *Bonne camarade*?'

'Oh, yes. . . . Oh, very, I should think.' She added: 'If

they weren't awfully kind people they wouldn't ask me to stay with them under the circumstances, would they?'

'No, naturally not.' Stephan answered with bitterness. 'Well, if she's as kind as all that, why don't you want to stay with her? You must go, Mado; it seems to me so much the best thing for you to do. Look here, you must go.'

'All right!' she said. She would have agreed to anything to quieten him and make him happier, and she was still full of the sense of the utter futility of all things.

As she walked back to the tram she wondered why she had ever thought the matter important at all. There was a merry-go-round at the Porte d'Orléans where the tram stopped. Children were being hoisted on to the backs of the gaily painted wooden horses. Then the music started to clank: '*Je vous aime*.' And the horses pranced around, pawing the air in a mettlesome way.

Marya stayed there for a long time watching a little frail, blonde girl, who careered past, holding tightly on to the neck of her steed, her face tense and strained with delight. The merry-go-round made her feel more normal, less like a grey ghost walking in a vague, shadowy world.

The day before Marya left the Hôtel de l'Univers she received a money order for five pounds from her aunt and namesake enclosed in a letter:

My dear Marya,

Your letter distressed me. You are rather vague — you always are a little vague, dear child. But I gather that all is not well with you. It is difficult for me to offer any advice, since you write so seldom and say so little when you do write. I feel that we live, and have lived for a long time, in different worlds. However, I send the money you ask for. I only wish it were at all possible to send more.

Is your husband well? You don't mention him. You have not quarrelled with him, I hope, or he with you. As I say, your letter distressed me and I feel so powerless to offer help of any sort.

Do write soon and tell me that things are going better with you.

Your affectionate aunt,
Maria Hughes.

P.S. Have you thought of visiting the British clergyman resident in Paris? He might be able to help you. There are, I believe, several. You could easily find out the address of one of them, or I could find out and send it to you.

8

AT NINE O'CLOCK every morning the *femme de ménage* tapped at the door of the little room where the grey and green striped curtains hung straightly over long windows, to announce that coffee was ready.

When Marya went down to the studio she would find Lois lying on the divan. Heidler sat in a big armchair near the stove opening his letters, and when the last letter was read he unfolded the *Matin* and asked for more coffee. Marya always brought the cup and the sugar, for he was very majestic and paternal in a dressing-gown, and it seemed natural that she should wait on him. He would thank her without looking at her and disappear behind the newspaper. He had abruptly become the remote impersonal male of the establishment.

The trio would lunch at Lefranc's, and as Lois had decided that she wished to begin her portrait of the sleeveless dress and the short black gloves at once, Marya spent long, calm afternoons staring through the windows at the tops of the leafless trees and listening to stories about Montparnasse. Lois wore a flowered overall and stood very straight as she worked, her chest well out, her round, brown eyes travelling rapidly from the sitter to the canvas and back again. The movement of her head was oddly like that of a bird picking up crumbs. She talked volubly. She would often stop painting to talk, and it was evident that she took Montparnasse very seriously indeed. She thought of it as a possible stepping-stone to higher things and she liked explaining, classifying, fitting the inhabitants (that is to say, of course, the Anglo-Saxon inhabitants) into their proper places in the scheme of things. The Beautiful Young Men, the Dazzlers, the Middle Westerners, the Down-and-Outs, the Freaks who never would do anything, the Freaks who just possibly might.

Sometimes she would ask questions, and Marya, longing to assert her point of view, would try to describe the charm of her life with Stephan. The vagabond nights, the fresh mornings, the long sleepy afternoons spent behind drawn curtains.

'Stephan's a – a vivid sort of person, you see. What a stupid word! I mean natural. Natural as an animal. He made me come alive; he taught me everything. I was happy. Sometimes just the way the light fell would make me unutterably happy.'

'Yes, of course,' Lois would say intelligently. 'I can quite see how he got hold of you. Quite.'

Lois was extremely intelligent. She held her head up. She looked at people with clear, honest eyes. She expressed well-read opinions about every subject under the sun in a healthy voice, and was so perfectly sure of all she said that it would have been a waste of time to contradict her. And, in spite of all this, or because of it, she gave a definite impression of being insensitive to the point of stupidity – or was it insensitive to the point of cruelty? Which? That was the question. But that, of course, always is the question.

Marya admired her benefactress, but the moment of soft intimacy had come and gone. She felt remote and lonely perched up on the model-stand, listening. Besides, after a time she began to feel that she knew all there was to be known about the various couples of Beautiful Young Men or the charm and chic of Plump Polly. The Beautiful Young Men undulated – they wore jerseys and *bérets basques*; they were spiteful and attractive and talented, and could be little English gentlemen when they liked.

'And that,' said Lois, 'is a very useful quality. In fact – call me a snob if you like – it's my favourite quality. That and good dancing. And, after all, you've got to be careful, haven't you? There's no knowing what you mightn't be let in for. There're some funny ones round here, I can tell you. Some of H. J.'s discoveries I wouldn't trust a yard.'

As for Plump Polly, a former Ziegfeld Folly, she, it seemed, had started a riot in the Dôme on the 14th of July.

'She got up on a bench and sang the Marseillaise. Oh, she was very serious, tears in her eyes and all that. All the Americans were delighted, but the French people thought that she was singing an English parody – well, you know what French people are sometimes. And it was the 14th of July. They broke a lot of glasses and things, and Plump Polly had to be hustled out of the back door by the *patron*.'

Lois also discussed Love, Childbirth (especially childbirth, for the subject fascinated her), Complexes, Paris, Men, Prostitution, and Sensitiveness, which she thought an unmitigated nuisance.

'Clergymen's daughters without any money. Long slim fingers and all the rest. What's the use of it? Those sort of people don't do any good in the world.'

'Well, don't worry,' answered Marya. 'They're getting killed off slowly.'

'Lois is as hard as nails,' she would find herself thinking. A sentence she had read somewhere floated fantastically into her mind: ' "It's so nice to think that the little thing enjoys it too," said the lady, watching her cat playing with a mouse.'

*

Every Thursday Lois gave a party, and Marya felt strangely at a loss during these gatherings where everyone seemed so efficient, so up and doing, so full of That Important Feeling and everything – even sin – was an affair of principle and uplift if you were an American, and of proving conclusively that you belonged to the upper classes, but were nevertheless an anarchist, if you were English. The women were long-necked and very intelligent and they would get into corners and say simple, truthful things about each other. Sometimes they were both intelligent and wealthy and would come to Montparnasse seeking cheap but effective protégés.

'Does that nice-looking young man write? Because if he does I might be able to help him. You know my Ting-a-Ling, Lois? Sweet thing! Well, the little woman who used to look after Ting-a-Ling writes. She writes poems. I got something of hers into our club magazine. Oh, well, then she got very careless and absent-minded and I found a flea on Ting. So I sent her off.'

Marya liked the parties best when, about midnight, everybody was a little drunk. She would watch Heidler, who could not dance, walking masterfully up and down the room to the strains of 'If you knew Susie as I know Susie' played on the gramophone, and wonder almost resentfully why his eyes were always so vague when he looked at her. His sidelong, cautious glances slid over her as it were.

'He looks very German,' she decided. But when they danced together she felt a definite sensation of warmth and pleasure.

*

Every Saturday Marya went to Fresnes and waited in the queue of poor and patient people till she saw Stephan, who, craning forward, would talk to her in a voice that seemed to be growing rusty. She thought of him jumping about to the orders of the fat red warder and felt repugnance, a pity which seemed as if it would break her heart, a dreadful, cold loneliness. She would go back to the studio and sit very silent with haunted eyes.

'D'you intend to go on doing this?' asked Lois one day.

Marya told her that she did.

'Well,' remarked Lois, 'I don't approve. The whole atmosphere of a place like that is awfully bad for you. Prisons . . .'

'Please,' said Marya, 'don't talk about it.'

She felt that it would be really unbearable to hear Lois talking common sense about prison and the punished in her young man's voice. Lois said that she intended to talk about it.

'Because I do feel so strongly – we both feel so strongly – that your only chance is to put the whole thing behind you and start again.'

'Start what?' asked Marya.

'You're a very tiresome child,' answered Lois. 'Very. You know that I'm pulling every string I can, and so's H. J.

We're certain to fix you up. For instance, I'm almost sure I could get you a mannequin job in about a month or six weeks at What's-his-name in the Rue Royale. You'll be all right,' she continued. 'You'll row your little boat along. You've got your own little charm, and so on.'

Marya looked up suddenly. There was something very like a menace in her long eyes. . . .

'Your own little charm and so on,' repeated Lois. 'But if you try to help your husband, you're done.'

Marya got up and walked to the window. She was crying, and Lois watched her with a puzzled expression, strangely without pity. She said:

'Lots of gels make extraordinary marriages, for all sorts of reasons. When a gel is really lonely and hasn't got a bean it's no use asking why she does things. But the time comes when, if you want to save yourself, you must cut loose. Can't you see that?'

'No, I can't,' said Marya. She repeated with violence: 'I can't. I don't think about things in that way.' Words that she longed to shout, to scream, crowded into her mind: 'You talk and you talk and you don't understand. Not anything. It's all false, all second-hand. You say what you've read and what other people tell you. You think you're very brave and sensible, but one flick of pain to yourself and you'd crumple up.'

She muttered: 'You don't understand.'

'Well, all right,' said Lois, 'let's talk about something else. Will you make me up for the Russian ball at the Bullier tomorrow? I'm going to wear a purple wig. . . . You know I hate myself made up. I don't think it's my genre, as they say here. But H. J. likes it. And I always give way to H. J. I give him what he wants until his mood changes. I found out long ago that that was the only way to manage him.' She suddenly looked complacent, smug, and very female and added: 'H. J.'s an autocrat, I can tell you.'

'Oh, is he?' said Marya vaguely. 'Yes, he is, I think.' She thought with horror: 'I do hope she isn't going to start talking about love and the pangs of childbirth.'

But Lois said: 'D'you mind going to the coiffeur's shop tomorrow to fetch the wig? I want to be quite sure to have it in time. It's a place in the Rue St Honoré.'

Marya answered that of course she would go.

She dined that night by herself in a little crêmerie in the Rue St Jacques. After the meal, which she paid for with her last carefully hoarded hundred franc note, she walked very quickly along the winding street, between two rows of gas-lamps, past the low doors of little buvettes, where a gramophone played gaily and workmen in caps stood drinking at the counters. It was a beautiful street. The street of home-less cats, she often thought. She never came into it without seeing several of them, prowling, thin vagabonds, furtive, aloof, but strangely proud. Sympathetic creatures, after all.

There was a smell of spring in the air. She felt unhappy, excited, strangely expectant. She tried – and failed – to imagine herself as a mannequin and she thought a great deal with deliberate gratitude about Lois. Lois in her most charming aspect, lying on the divan in the morning pouring out coffee, soft and lazy in a fragile dressing-gown, her beautiful strong arms bare to the shoulder. The next night she waited eagerly on Lois dressing for the dance and spent half an hour carefully making her up. Ochre powder, a little rouge, the tips of the ears, just under the eyes. Huge, sombre eyes and a red mouth – that's what she was getting at. Lois sat before the mirror in the studio. The light was so much better there.

'You ought always to do it,' said Heidler, looking at his wife with interest.

'Do you think so?' answered Lois. She pulled on the purple wig carefully. Her reddened mouth looked extraordinarily hard, Marya thought. When she was following Lois into the bedroom: 'No, sit down for a minute,' Heidler said. 'What a fidget you are!'

He wore spectacles. She thought that he looked kinder, older, less German.

'Don't rush off,' he said. And then, 'Oh, God, I am so utterly sick of myself sometimes. D'you ever get sick of yourself? No, not yet, of course. Wait a bit, you will one of these days.'

'No,' answered Marya reflectively. 'I'm not sick of myself. I'm rather sick of my sort of life.'

'Well, I'm sick of myself,' Heidler said gloomily. 'And yet it goes on. One knows that the whole damn thing's idiotic, futile, not even pleasant, but one goes on. One's caught in a sort of trap, I suppose.'

He stared at the ground between his big knees.

9

THE SPRING came early that year and very suddenly. So that one day the branches of the trees in the Luxembourg Gardens were bare and grim and the next they waved cool leaves in a kind wind. Or so it seemed. Then the chestnuts flowered and the girls walking along with linked arms began to discuss their new clothes endlessly. '*Ma robe verte* . . . *mon costume gris.* . . .' And on the Boulevard St Michel bevies of young men of every nationality under the sun strolled along smiling at every woman they passed. The Latins were gay and insolent, the Northerns lustful, shamefaced and condescending, the Easterns shy, curious and contemptuous.

Nearly every week-end the Heidlers went down to a country cottage they had found near Brunoy on the way to Fontainebleau. Twice Marya went with them.

Left alone at the flat in the Avenue de l'Observatoire she would dine in the Rue St Jacques and go for solitary walks when the meal was over. But she vaguely disliked the Boulevard St Michel with its rows of glaring cafés, and always felt relieved when she turned into the Boulevard Montparnasse, softer, more dimly lit, more kindly. There she could plunge herself into her dream.

Fancy being shut up in a little dark dirty cell when the spring was coming. Perhaps one morning you'd smell it through the window and then surely your heart would nearly burst with the longing for liberty.

One evening, just outside the Café de la Rotonde, she met Miss De Solla. That lady had been ill, and seemed discontented with Montparnasse. She was going to Florence for some months, she said, and would not be back in Paris before June.

When Marya informed her that she was living with the Heidlers: 'Yes,' said Miss De Solla, with an uneasy expression, 'as a matter of fact, I heard that you were.'

She added: 'I must be getting along.'

10

THE BAL DU PRINTEMPS is a small, dingy café in the Rue Mouffetard. There is a long zinc bar where the clients can drink a peaceful apéritif after the day's work. There are painted wooden tables, long wooden benches and a small gallery where the band sits – a concertina, a flute and a violin. The couples dance in a cleared space at the end of the room. Men in caps and hatless girls cling together, shake themselves and turn with abandon and a certain amount of genuine enjoyment.

Two policemen at the door supervise the proceedings, and there is a large placard on the wall:

'*Une tenue correcte est rigoureusement exigée.*'

The Bal du Printemps is a family ball. If you want something *louche* you walk further on and turn twice to the left. Mr Rolls, the author, always hired this place for his weekly parties. Sometimes in the midst of the proceedings the surprised head of one of the usual clients would be thrust into the doorway. The landlord would shrug, wink, gesticulate, explain, and the pale youth would disappear, muttering something like: '*Mince de poules de luxe!*' But the quality of the brandy left a great deal to be desired. Imagining that it was very weak, people drank a good deal of it, and it generally had a very bad effect on their tempers.

Midnight. The band struck up *Valencia* for the sixth time.

Somebody said to somebody else: 'It's all very well to talk about Jew noses, but have you ever tried to paint your own mouth?'

The artist addressed burst into tears.

'He's only trying to be modern and brutal and all that, poor dear,' said her friend. . . . 'Don't mind him.'

'*Fine à l'eau*,' bawled a tall dark gentleman immediately in Mr Rolls's ear.

'Don't shout in my ear,' said Mr Rolls irritably.

'Well, get out of the way,' said the tall dark gentleman. 'Always blocking up the bar.'

'It's my bar,' remarked Mr Rolls with majesty.

'Then you ought to give your clients a chance,' said the other.

Mr Rolls wandered about, asking: 'Who brought that chap? How did that chap get in here? Who on earth is that chap?' Nobody knew. It did not matter.

An unknown lady seated herself at the end of one of the benches and remarked to Marya:

'Doesn't Swansee Grettle look awful tonight?'

'She looks,' said the unknown lady, smiling slowly, 'like a hundred gone bad, don't you think?' She was very healthy looking, was the unknown lady, with long, very sharp teeth.

How terrifying human beings were, Marya thought. But she had drunk two fines and a half-bottle of something which the *patron* of the Bal du Printemps called champagne, and after all it was a lovely party. Then she saw Lois standing near the doorway with her coat on. She beckoned and Marya got up with reluctance. It was only just half-past twelve.

'H. J.'s had enough of this,' said Lois. 'He wants to be taken home. D'you mind walking?'

'Not a bit,' answered Marya.

They went arm in arm through the lovely, crooked, silent streets. As they passed a little café on the Boulevard St Michel: 'This place is still open,' remarked Heidler. 'Let's have a bock.'

Lois said that she was tired.

'I'm going home. Don't be too long, you two.'

She disengaged herself, and walked on so abruptly that Marya stood looking after her with some astonishment.

'Come along,' said Heidler.

It was warm as a night in summer – a wonderfully still and brooding night. A sleepy waiter appeared with two glasses of beer and placed them on the only table left on the terrace.

'Do you know why Lois has gone off?' asked Heidler.

'No,' said Marya. 'Why?'

He spoke slowly, without looking at her:

'She's gone away to leave us together – to give me a chance to talk to you, d'you see? She knows that I'm dying with love for you, burnt up with it, tortured with it. That's why she's gone off.'

He had tilted his hat to the back of his head and was looking fixedly across the deserted street. He looked much younger, she thought, and extraordinarily hard.

'You think I'm drunk, don't you?' he said.

'Yes,' she told him. 'Of course.' She repeated: 'Of course. And I'm tired, so let's go home.'

'Do you know why your door is open every morning?'

asked Heidler. 'Have you noticed that it's open? No? Stay where you are and listen to what I've got to say. I've had enough. Now you've got to listen. Your door is open because I come up every night and open it. Then I look at you and go away again. One does meaningless things like that when one is tortured by desire. Don't you know that I wanted you the first time I saw you?' He nodded. 'Yes. Dare say that you didn't know.'

She stared at him, silent.

'Lois knows it now, anyway. . . . Well, I kept off you, didn't I? I knew that I could have you by putting my hand out, and I kept off you. I thought it wouldn't be playing the game. But there comes a limit, you see. There comes a limit to everything. I've been watching you; I watched you tonight and now I know that somebody else will get you if I don't. You're that sort.'

She said: 'You're abominably rude and unkind and unfair. And you're stupid in a lot of ways. Too stupid to realize how unfair you are.'

'Don't be silly,' he told her calmly. 'You've every right to be like that if you want to be like that, and I've every right to take advantage of it if I want to. That's truth, and all the rest is sob stuff.'

She thought: 'Sob stuff, sex stuff. That's the way men talk. And they look at you with hard, greedy eyes. I hate them with their greedy eyes.' She felt despair and a sort of hard rage. 'It's all wrong,' she thought. 'Everything's wrong.'

'Talk!' she said rudely. 'Talk. I'm going.'

She got up. He left money on the table, followed her and took her arm in his. When he touched her she felt warm and secure, then weak and so desolate that tears came into her eyes.

'It's all right, it's all right!' said Heidler soothingly.

The street was quite empty, a long street glistening with light like a sheet of water. Their footsteps echoed mournfully.

When they reached the studio:

'So you think I'm drunk,' said Heidler. 'So I am. So are you. But I'll talk to you tomorrow when I'm not drunk.'

Marya bolted the door of her room, collapsed on the bed and undressed dizzily and with difficulty. The nasal music of the concertina of the *bal musette* was still in her ears. 'I love you' they played, and *Valencia* and *Mon Paris*. The sound was still in her ears. And the voice of that little funny man. What was his name? The little sculptor. 'You're a victim. There's no endurance in your face. Victims are necessary so that the strong may exercise their will and become more strong.'

'I shall have to go away,' she decided. 'Of course. Naturally.'

Sleep was like falling into a black hole.

*

Next morning she woke early and lay watching the wind blow the striped curtain outwards. It was like the sail of a ship, she thought. Voices, steps, a knock on the door. She held her breath.

Lois called: 'Still asleep, Mado?'

'No, but I'm tired. I don't want any coffee. I've promised to lunch with Cairn.'

'Oh, all right, then,' said Lois.

Marya did not get up till after she heard the sound of the front-door being shut.

It was a cloudless, intoxicating day. The light pale gold, the sky silvery blue, the breeze sweet and fresh as if it blew up from the sea.

A tram-car lumbered past her, and she began to think of the women who stood in the queue at the prison of Fresnes and of the way they would edge forward mechanically and uselessly, pushing her as they edged. So that she was always forced to stand touching their musty clothes and their unwashed bodies. She remembered her tears and her submissions and the long hours she had spent walking between two rows of street lamps, solitary, possessed by pity as by a devil. 'I've been wasting my life,' she thought. 'How have I stood it for so long?'

And her longing for joy, for any joy, for any pleasure was a mad thing in her heart. It was sharp like pain and she clenched her teeth. It was like some splendid caged animal roused and fighting to get out. It was an unborn child jumping, leaping, kicking at her side.

*

'You're very late,' said Cairn, who was waiting for her in a restaurant in the Place Pigalle. 'I thought you weren't coming.'

He looked solemnly through his horn spectacles at her as she explained that she had walked part of the way, agreed that it was a lovely day and invited her to have a cocktail.

74

'Olives?'

He was an American, a writer of short stories; ugly, broad-shouldered, long-legged, slim-hipped.

'I thought you weren't coming,' said Cairn, and added astonishingly: 'I thought Heidler would stop you.'

Marya asked why he should stop her.

'Because he is a . . . oh, well, doesn't matter.'

'But he's very kind,' said Marya.

There was a question in her voice, for she felt a great longing to hear Heidler spoken of. She would have discussed Heidler with pleasure throughout the entire meal.

'Kind?' said Cairn. 'Heidler kind? My God!'

'Don't you think he's kind?' she persisted childishly.

'Don't let's talk about him,' said Cairn impatiently. 'What's he matter, anyway?'

'No,' said Marya, with regret, 'don't let's talk about him.' She added: 'They've been nice to me, you know, wonderfully nice.'

'Have they?'

He flashed a quick, curious look from under the spectacles, hesitated, then said:

'Ah, Marya mia . . . Well, that's all right, then.'

They talked about Cairn's new hat — whether it was or was not too small for him, and about a short story that he wished to write and about money.

'Haven't any,' said Cairn gloomily.

Then they talked about Life.

'It frightens me,' said Marya. But as they drank their coffee, she said to him: 'Cairn, isn't not caring a damn a nice feeling?'

'Of course it is,' said Cairn cheerfully. 'You've got to be

75

an *arriviste* or a *je m'en fichiste* in this life.' He added: 'Only, of course, if you are going to be a *je m'en fichiste*, you must have the nerve to stand the racket afterwards, because there always is a racket, you know.'

'Yes, I know,' said Marya. 'I've found that out already.'

*

It was late when she got back to the Avenue de l'Observatoire. When she looked up from the street the windows were in darkness, but as soon as she opened the door Heidler called out from the studio:

'Hullo! There you are! You're late. Did you enjoy yourself?'

'Yes, very much,' said Marya.

He got up and turned on one of the lights, but the room was still full of shadows. He looked tired.

'After all, he's quite old,' she thought and faced him, feeling ironical and defiant.

'I love you,' said Heidler. 'I love you, my dear, I love you. And I wish I were dead. For God's sake, be a little kind to me. Oh, you cold and inhuman devil!'

'I'm not cold,' answered Marya.

Suddenly she was full of a great longing to explain herself.

'H. J., I want to be happy. Oh, I want it so badly. You don't know how badly. I don't want to be hurt. I don't want anything black or miserable or complicated any more. I want to be happy, I want to play around and have good times like – like other people do. . . . Oh, do leave me alone. I'm so scared of being unhappy.'

76

'You've got a fear complex,' remarked Heidler, 'that's what's the matter with you.'

'I don't want to be hurt any more,' she told him in a low voice. 'If I'm hurt again I shall go mad. You don't know. . . . How can you know? I can't stand any more, I won't stand it.'

'Rubbish!' said Heidler tenderly. 'Rubbish!'

'You don't know anything about me,' she went on fiercely. 'Nothing! You can't lay down the law about me because you don't know anything.'

'But I want to make you happy,' he exclaimed loudly. 'It's my justification that I want to. And that I will, d'you hear? In spite of you, I'll do it!'

'Yes?' said Marya. 'And what about Lois?'

Heidler leaned back in his chair, crossed his legs, cleared his throat.

'My dear,' he remarked, 'you don't understand Lois.'

'Don't I?' asked Marya.

'Not a bit. Lois,' he went on, speaking carefully and persuasively, 'is not an excitable person.'

'I've gathered that much,' remarked Marya dryly.

'You are so excitable yourself,' declared Heidler. 'You tear yourself to pieces over everything and, of course, your fantastic existence has made you worse. You simply don't realize that most people take things calmly. Most people don't tear themselves to bits. They have a sense of proportion and so on. Lois and I each go our own way and that's been the arrangement for some time, if you want to know. Why, look here; do you know what she said about you a few days ago? I tell you because I want you to realize that Lois simply doesn't come into this at all between you

77

and me. . . . She said: "The matter with Mado is that she's too virtuous".' He nodded. 'Yes, that's what she said; that's what she thinks about the situation.'

'Oh, is that so?' Marya spoke thoughtfully.

He asked her if she couldn't understand that all that didn't matter.

'I want to comfort you. I want to hold you tight – and safe – d'you see. Safe!'

'H. J., don't.' She put her hand up to her mouth as if to hide her lips. 'Oh, well! Give me a cigarette, will you, please?'

'You smoke too much,' he told her irritably. 'I'm never alone with you, never. And if I'm alone with you for five minutes, you smoke or you paint your mouth or you perform some other monkey trick of the sort – instead of listening to me. Lois will come in, in a minute.'

'She is in,' said Marya; 'I heard her some time ago.'

'Oh, is she?' He hesitated, looked at Marya, went out of the room.

She drew her feet up on to the sofa, clasped her hands around her knees and stared fixedly in front of her.

I I

LOIS CAME INTO the room carrying a small flowered paper bag. 'Hello, Mado, why are you sitting in this half-darkness?' She put on the light near the door. 'I've been running round the shops all the afternoon. I've bought you this to cheer your black dress up.'

She opened the paper bag and took out a lace collar, touching it with careful fingers.

'Thank you,' said Marya in a low voice.

Lois went on: 'I'm going to dine with Maurice and Anna. And I'm late. I must fly.' Her eyes, which were swollen as if she had been crying, travelled restlessly round the room. 'Get H. J. to take you somewhere. He'll be here in a minute; he's gone for some cigarettes.' She turned to walk out of the room.

'Lois!' said Marya. And stopped breathless.

'Well, what is it?'

'I want to talk to you.'

'Won't tomorrow do?' Lois asked coldly. 'I'm really in an awful hurry. I don't want to keep Anna waiting.'

'Well, it needn't be a long conversation,' Marya told her. 'I want to go, and the sooner the better, don't you think so? I must ask you to lend me a hundred francs because I haven't any money left at all. I'll go at once, and you can tell H. J. that I insisted on it.'

All the time that she spoke she was thinking: 'This is

perfectly useless. She doesn't believe a word I'm saying. She hates me. She's going to try to down me. Whatever I do, she'll hate me and try to down me.'

'Don't be silly, Mado,' said Lois uncertainly. She looked at Marya with the painfully intent expression of a slow brained person who is trying to think quickly.

'What's her game? What's she up to? I must be clever and try to find out what she's up to.'

'Of course, you can't go.'

'And why not?'

'Well,' asked Lois, 'where would you go to?' Her brown eyes were suspicious, troubled like pools when the mud beneath has been stirred up.

'When I say: go off,' said Marya, 'I mean, go right off.'

They watched each other cautiously and steadily for some moments. Then Lois sat down in the chair facing the divan and remarked with calmness:

'All this, of course, is because H. J.'s been making love to you, I know. I was listening just now, if it comes to that. Well,' she added defiantly, 'in my place you'd have done the same thing.'

'No,' said Marya.

'No?' echoed Lois unbelievingly.

'I might come into the room and make a hell of a scene, but I'd never listen at the door, because I've not got patience enough. We're different people, Lois.'

'Yes,' agreed Lois reluctantly. 'I suppose we are. But that's no reason why we should quarrel, is it?'

She began to fidget nervously with the fastening of her handbag.

'I don't see what good it will do if you go off. It seems

such a pity to smash up all our plans for you, just because H. J. imagines that he's in love with you – for the minute.' She went on in a reflective voice: 'Of course, mind you, he wants things badly when he does want them. He's a whole hogger'.

'So am I,' Marya told her. 'That's just why I must go off.'

The other made an impatient and expressive gesture, as if to say: 'D'you suppose that I care what you are, or think or feel? I'm talking about the man, the male, the important person, the only person who matters.'

'He's a whole hogger,' Lois repeated, 'and if you go away now he'll go after you. That's what he'll do.'

'It's fatal making a fuss,' she muttered. 'The more fuss one makes . . . I don't believe in making scenes about things, forcing things. I believe in letting things alone. I hate scenes.'

She stopped. All day she had tormented herself and now she was on the brink of an abyss of sincerity. She twisted her hands in her lap, thinking: Oh, no, my girl, you won't go away. You'll stay here where I can keep an eye on you. It won't last long . . . It can't last long. I've always let him alone and given him what he wanted and it's never failed me. It won't fail me now. He'll get tired of her as soon as she gives in. Pretty! She's revolting. You can see when you look at her that she's been chewed up. God! what have I done to be worried like this? Didn't I try to do a decent thing? This is the result; this is what I get for it.

She said bitterly: 'Of course, I was a fool to have you here, only a fool like me would have done a thing like that, but I don't see what good your going away now will do.'

Her eyes, when she looked at Marya, were hard, false, questioning. It was as if she were observing some strange animal that might be dangerous, debating the best method of dealing with it.

'I tell you that I'll go off,' said Marya. 'Tonight, if you like. Right off. What more can I do? I won't see H. J. again.'

('Come, come,' answered Lois's eyes. 'As woman to woman, do you suppose I believe that?')

'Well, it's very dramatic and generous of you and all that,' she remarked. 'Why don't you talk it over with him? I should if I were you. As far as I'm concerned, I don't see any reason why you should go. I don't want to send you away and then have it on my conscience that you've gone to the devil and all that. Well, that's what you said, that you didn't care what happened to you. I thought that a dreadful thing.'

Her voice was so prim that Marya began to laugh, suddenly and loudly. Lois stared at her, got up, went to the looking-glass, arranged her side-locks carefully, and continued in a calm voice:

'We're making a great fuss about nothing at all, aren't we? Drama is catching, I find. In any case, you can't go tonight.'

Marya asked abruptly: 'Tell me, did you really say that what is the matter with me is that I am too virtuous?'

'Well, all this looks rather like it, doesn't it?' Lois answered. 'You must be rather worried about your virtue if you want to rush off at a minute's notice. Look here, I must be off; I'm horribly late.'

At the door she turned suddenly: 'What? What did you say?' she asked.

'Nothing.' Marya lay back and shut her eyes.

Lois was a shadow, less than a shadow. Lois had simply ceased to exist.

The front door banged.

Marya lay very still listening to the hooting of the cars outside. She felt sharply alive but very tired, so languid as to be almost incapable of movement. A profound conviction of the unreality of everything possessed her. She thought: 'I wonder if taking opium is like this?'

*

'Hullo, H. J.,' she said, and sat up quickly. He was too formidable standing over her. 'Listen. I've been telling Lois that I want to go – I think I'd better.'

'Oh, I think I'd better. I think I'd better,' she kept on saying in a little, pitiful voice; but when he took her in his arms she thought: 'How gentle he is. I was lost before I knew him. All my life before I knew him was like being lost on a cold, dark night.'

She shivered. Then she smiled and shut her eyes again.

He whispered: 'I love you, I love you. What did you say?'

'That you don't understand.'

'Oh, yes, I do, my dear,' said Heidler. 'Oh, yes, I do.'

12

THE THREE DINED together at Lefranc's the next evening. They sat, as usual, at a table in a little alcove at the end of the room, and Monsieur Lefranc (also as usual) hovered about them attentively. Monsieur Lefranc admired Lois Heidler. He considered her a good-looking woman, a sensible, tidy, well-dressed woman who knew how to appreciate food. Marya he distrusted, and he had told his wife so more than once. 'And who is she, that one?' he would say. On this particular evening, then, he served first the soup and then the fish with his own hands and asked:

'*Ça vous plait, Madame Heidler?*'

'Oh, very nice, very nice,' answered Lois.

Then Monsieur Lefranc cast one astute glance at her deeply circled eyes, another at Marya's reflection in the glass and told himself: '*Ça y est.* I knew it! Ah, the *grue!*' So he waited on Lois with sympathy and gentleness; he waited on Marya grimly, and when he looked at Heidler, his expression said: 'Come, come, my dear sir. As man to man, what a mistake you're making!'

Madame Lefranc, from behind her bar, was also watching the trio with interest and curiosity. But she beamed on Marya every bit as kindly as she beamed on Lois, for she was a plump and placid woman who never took sides, and when her husband (a very moral man) judged a female client with severity, she would often say: 'Life is very droll. One never knows, Josef, one never knows.'

Marya was unconscious of Monsieur Lefranc's hostility. She was absorbed, happy, without thought for perhaps the first time in her life. No past. No future. Nothing but the present: the flowers on the table, the taste of wine in her mouth. She glanced at the rough texture of Heidler's coat-sleeve and longed to lay her face against it.

Lois, however, instantly reacting to the atmosphere of sympathy and encouragement, sat very straight, dominating the situation and talking steadily in a cool voice.

'We must get Mado another hat, H. J.'

Heidler looked sideways at Marya cautiously and critically.

'She must be chic,' his wife went on. 'She must do us credit.' She might have been discussing the dressing of a doll.

'Let's go to Luna-park after dinner,' she said. 'We'll put Mado on the joy wheel, and watch her being banged about a bit. Well, she ought to amuse us sometimes; she ought to sing for her supper; that's what she's here for, isn't it?'

Heidler's face was expressionless. It was impossible to tell whether this badinage amused or annoyed him.

'Well, shall we go to Luna-park?' persisted Lois.

'No,' answered Heidler reflectively. 'No, I don't think so.'

Lois said in a high, excited voice that she was bored to death with Montparnasse.

'I'm bored, bored, bored! Look here. Let's go to a music-hall, the *promenoir* of a music-hall, that's what I feel like. Something *canaille*, what?'

*

Two naked girls were dancing before a background of blue and mauve which was like a picture by Marie Laurencin.

'If they'd only keep still,' Marya thought. 'They would be awfully nice if they were perfectly still.'

But the girls hopped with persistence. She looked away from the stage at an enormously stout lady promenading in a black and salmon georgette dress. The lady was worth watching. She had the head of a Roman emperor and she paced up and down with great dignity, glancing at various men with a good-natured but relentless expression.

The two girls having pranced smilingly off the stage, the curtain fell and rose again on the Spanish singer who was the star of the evening: a slim creature in a black crinoline gown, who wore her hair swept away from her face and ears. She was charming. She was like some frail and passionate child, and she sang her songs simply in a sweet, small voice.

'Oh, what a darling!' said Marya after the first song. But Lois ejaculated at intervals:

'Oh, very disappointing. Most!' and finally announced that she wanted to go to the Select bar (the Montparnasse one) and eat a Welsh rarebit.

That night the place seemed to be full of red-haired ladies in *robes de style*. Mr Blinks, the brilliant American, was balancing himself on a stool at one end of the bar. Guy Lester was at the other end, very drunk. All the dear old familiar faces, as Lois said.

'But a bit pink-eyed. Or are they not? Perhaps I just think they are because I'm in a bad temper.' She began to disparage the Spaniard at length: 'Not half fine gel enough, was she?'

'Did you like her, Mado?' asked Heidler.

'Yes, I did, very much.'

'Oh, charming!' said Lois. Her voice went up a semi-tone. 'But small, small. I liked the dancers rather.'

Marya remarked in a cold, hostile way that she thought the dancers were bouncers.

'Hate bouncers!'

'I don't see,' went on Lois, 'what the girl was driving at, myself. She tries to get an atmosphere of fate and terror. The weak creature doomed and all that – such nonsense. And, besides, she doesn't do it. That song where she stabbed her lover, for instance. You don't stab a man with a little feeble gesture and a sweet and simple smile.'

Heidler said: 'Lois doesn't believe in fate, and she doesn't approve of weakness.'

'Oh, it's a damn convenient excuse sometimes,' answered Lois. The two women stared coldly at each other.

'After all,' remarked Marya suddenly, 'weak, weak, how does anybody really know who's weak and who isn't? You don't need to be a fine bouncing girl to stab anybody, either. The will to stab would be the chief thing, I should think.'

Heidler coughed.

'Have some more stout,' he said; 'have another Welsh rarebit.' He added with relief: 'Come along over here, Guy.'

Guy, who was a tall and beautiful and willowy young man, came along. He fixed a severe, slightly bleared blue eye on Marya and declared that he thought she was a hussy. He was very drunk.

'I'm young and innocent,' said Guy, 'but I know a hussy when I see one.'

'Darling Marya,' said Lois, laughing on a high note. 'You don't know her, you don't. She's as harmless as they're made, Guy. A sweet young thing on the sentimental side.'

'And one word to you both,' thought Marya. The music-hall had excited her. She felt pugnacious. She sat silent with a sullen, resentful expression on her face. From time to time Heidler looked at her under his eyebrows with clever, cautious eyes.

Lois began: 'There was a young woman called Marya. Who thought, "But I must have a caree – er." ' And so on and so on. . . .

They walked home along the street which runs close to the Luxembourg Gardens, empty, silent and enchanted in the darkness.

'Good night, you two,' said Lois when they got to the studio. She went to her room and locked the door.

*

'H.J.,' said Marya. 'It's no use. I can't go on with this. I can't stick it. It isn't my line at all.'

'But that's not playing the game, is it?' remarked Heidler, in an impersonal voice. 'Not any sort of game.'

'What game?' answered Marya fiercely. 'Your game? Lois's game? Why should I play Lois's game? Yes, that is just it, it's all a game I can't play, that I don't know how to play.'

He said: 'You're making a stupid mistake, a really tragic mistake about Lois. I tell you that you misunderstand her utterly. You will persist in judging us by the standards of the awful life you've lived. Can't you understand that you are in a different world now? People breed differently after a while, you know. You won't be let down. There's no trick, no trap. You're with friends. And look here, my dear, what's the use of starting this conversation at this time of night? We'll talk about it tomorrow. Lois doesn't want to be given away; she doesn't want anybody to know, and I assure you that that's all she cares about. Of course, she'll be furious if anybody knows, and that's why if you go off in a hurry you will make things difficult for me. I beg you not to make things so difficult for me.'

She felt hypnotized as she listened to him, impotent.

As she lay in bed she longed for her life with Stephan as one longs for vanished youth. A gay life, a carefree life just wiped off the slate as it were. Gone! A horrible nostalgia, an ache for the past seized her.

Nous n'irons plus au bois;
Les lauriers sont coupés. . . .

Gone, and she was caught in this appalling muddle. Life was like that. Here you are, it said, and then immediately afterwards. Where are you? Her life, at any rate, had always been like that.

'Of course,' she told herself, 'I ought to clear out.'

But when she thought of an existence without Heidler her heart turned over in her side and she felt sick.

A board creaked outside.

She watched the handle of the door turning very gently, very slowly. And during the few moments that passed from the time she heard the board creak to the time she saw Heidler and said, 'Oh, it's you then, it's you,' she was in a frenzy of senseless fright. Fright of a child shut up in a dark room. Fright of an animal caught in a trap.'

'What is it? What is it, then?' whispered Heidler. 'My darling! There, there, there!'

13

ONE AFTERNOON AT the end of April, whilst sitting in the Café du Dôme, drinking a gin and vermouth, Cairn, that imaginative and slightly sentimental young man, wrote the following pneumatique to Marya.

Mon vieux,

I haven't met you for an age. Can you come to August's for lunch tomorrow — Saturday, one o'clock? Do. I'll be tickled to death to see you.

Yours,

Cairn

Then, full of imaginative and slightly sentimental resolution, he went out and posted the pneumatique. 'For,' thought he, 'that girl's not getting a fair deal.'

However, throughout luncheon with Marya, he felt doubtful, cautious and somewhat embarrassed. That day she was not so pretty as he remembered her. 'After all,' he told himself, 'I've got no money. I can't do anything for her. She probably knows perfectly well what she's up to, and can bargain while the bargaining's good.'

'Shall we drink Burgundy?'

'Yes, let's,' said Marya.

He wondered if she knew the sort of thing people were saying about her, and decided she probably did because her mouth was so hard and her eyes were so sad. Lost she looked. L'Enfant Perdu or The Babe in the Wood. Something like that. And she was the type he liked, too. Not a beautiful specimen of the type, of course.

After the meal was over: 'Let's go and have coffee at the Closerie des Lilas.'

'Yes, do let's,' said Marya.

It was a sunny day and they sat on the terrace. Cairn sneezed and she started so violently that half her coffee was spilt over into the saucer.

'Nerves, nerves,' said Cairn. 'Now then, what's the matter? Something's the matter; you're not looking well.'

She told him irritably: 'Don't poor-little-thing me. I can't stand it this morning.'

'You ought to be talked to sensibly,' said Cairn. 'Why have you got to look so peaky all of a sudden?'

'Because I hate trailing about with the Heidlers.'

He said 'Oh!' and looked taken aback.

'I don't care,' said Marya, 'what it sounds like. There's the truth.'

Cairn's little twinkling eyes behind his spectacles were suddenly very wary. Of course he was a clever young man, but how clever, that was the question. Clever enough to recognize the truth when he heard it? Hardly anybody was clever enough for that. People went ludicrously wrong. You told the truth, the stark truth – or perhaps you gave it a fig-leaf so as not to harrow too much – and everybody said: 'Come, come,' and 'Don't tell me,' and: 'Do you think I was born yesterday?' You told lies and they said: 'Ah, the *cri du cœur*!' Supposing that she said: 'Very well then, I will tell you. Listen. Heidler thinks he loves me and I love him. Terribly. I don't like him or trust him. I love him. D'you get me? And Lois says that she doesn't mind a bit and gives us her blessing – the importance of sex being vastly exaggerated and any little thing like that. But she says that I mustn't give her away. So does Heidler. They call that playing the game. So I have to trail around with them. And she takes it out of me all the time in all sorts of ways. I can just keep my end up now, but soon I won't be able to. And then, you see, I'm conscience-stricken about her. I'm horribly sorry for her. But I know that she hasn't a spark of pity for me. She's just out to down me—and she will.'

Supposing that she said all that to this calm, clever young man? No, his eyes were too cautious. He wouldn't be clever enough, she decided. Besides, one didn't say that sort of thing.

He was asking her reasonably why she didn't go off if she was not happy.

'Because I haven't anywhere else to go. Oh, don't let's talk about it. I realize what a feeble excuse that is. Besides, it isn't the real excuse.'

Cairn said slowly that it wasn't so feeble as all that.

'Not for a woman, anyway.'

'For a woman – for a woman. Why this sudden tenderness for the female sex? But, my poor dear,' she mocked, 'you're positively rococo, as what's-her-name would say.'

'Oh, it's a sad world!' grumbled Cairn. 'Sometimes it's so difficult to know what the hell to say.'

'Don't say anything,' she told him firmly.

'Look here,' he said, 'I'll say this much anyhow. I haven't got any money myself, as you know, but I'll borrow five hundred francs for you. It's not much, but, after all, you can live in the Dôme on coffee and croissants for quite a long time on that. Besides, when I get back to America I'll probably be able to send you some more. Heidler is a humbug,' he added violently, 'and God help you if you don't see it.'

'You think so?' asked Marya.

'I don't think; I know, and as for Mrs Heidler . . .'

'She hates me,' said Marya in a low voice.

'Of course she hates you,' Cairn replied impatiently. 'What do you expect? She'd be a very unnatural woman if she didn't hate you.'

'But I don't mind her hating me,' continued Marya. 'What I mind is that she pretends she doesn't.'

'That,' said Cairn, 'is what is known here as a *moyen classique.*'

'So it's as obvious as all that?' asked Marya after a silence.

'Oh, yes, it's fairly obvious.'

Cairn looked away with an embarrassed, even alarmed expression, fidgeted and cleared his throat.

'I must go,' she told him. 'I'm going to meet Heidler.'

'Oh, are you?' said Cairn, looking grim.

'Yes, at St Julien le Pauvre. He wants to show it to me.'

'He would,' muttered Cairn; 'he would choose a church for a background. Oh, my God!'

But Marya had decided that Cairn couldn't help her. He only added a sharp edge to her obsession.

'You'll come on Tuesday?' said Cairn, still with that air of being exceedingly embarrassed.

'Yes,' she said absently.

There he was, incapable of helping.

Before she had walked three steps from the Closerie des Lilas she had forgotten all about him.

*

The church was very cool and dark-shadowed, when they came in out of the sun. It smelled of candles and incense and ancient prayers. Marya stood for a long time staring at the tall Virgin and wondered why she suggested not holiness but rather a large and peaceful tolerance of sin. We are all miserable sinners and the dust of the earth. A little more or a little less, a dirty glass or a very dirty glass, as Heidler would say . . .

'And you don't suppose that it matters to me,' said the tall Virgin smiling so calmly above her candles and flowers.

Marya turned to watch Heidler go down on one knee and cross himself as he passed the altar. He glanced quickly sideways at her as he did it, and she thought: 'I'll never be able to pray again now that I've seen him do that. Never! However sad I am.' And she felt very desolate.

*

'Hep!' shouted Heidler to a passing taxi. 'Get in. Look here,' he said, 'I don't want you to see Cairn again.'

'All right,' answered Marya.

His hand was over hers. Peace had descended on her and to that peace she was ready to sacrifice Cairn or anybody or anything.

'But I promised to lunch with him on Tuesday.'

'Well, write and say that you can't come. You must cut Cairn right out, you see.'

'Very well. I'm sorry, because I think he's kind; I like him.'

'He's hysterical,' said Heidler contemptuously.

The taxi jolted onwards.

'We want you to come down to Brunoy with us this afternoon.'

'Oh, no,' she told him hastily, 'I don't want to come.'

'But you must come. You're not looking well. We both think you need a change. What's the matter?'

'Nothing.'

'Why did you stiffen all over like that? Can't you come just to please me? Can't you not go to Fresnes for once?'

'Yes,' she said. And stopped herself from saying: 'I'll do anything to please you – anything.'

'What were you praying about just now?' she asked him suddenly.

'You!' he said.

'God's quite a pal of yours?'

'Yes,' said Heidler.

14

THEY SAT FACING her in the railway carriage and she looked at them with calmness, clear-sightedly, freed for one moment from her obsessions of love and hatred. They were so obviously husband and wife, so suited to each other, they were even in some strange way a little alike. 'Every pot has its lid,' says the French proverb, or perhaps Belgian – but French or Belgan, it's a good proverb.

Lois sat sturdily, with her knees, as usual, a little apart; her ungloved hands were folded over a huge leather handbag; on her dark face was the expression of the woman who is wondering how she is going to manage about the extra person to dinner. She probably was wondering just that. Her adequately becoming and expensive hat was well pulled down over her eyes. Her beige coat was well cut. Obviously of the species wife.

There she was: formidable, very formidable, an instrument made, exactly shaped and sharpened for one purpose. She didn't analyse; she didn't react violently; she didn't go in for absurd generosities or pities. Her motto was: 'I don't think women ought to make nuisances of themselves. I don't make a nuisance of myself; I grin and bear it, and I think that other women ought to grin and bear it, too.'

And there he was, like the same chord repeated in a lower key, sitting with his hands clasped in exactly the same posture as hers. Only his eyes were different. He could dream, that one. But his dreams would not be many-coloured, or dark shot with flame like Marya's. No, they'd be cold, she thought, or gross at moments. Almost certainly gross with those pale blue, secretive eyes. It seemed to her that, staring at the couple, she had hypnotized herself into thinking, as they did, that her mind was part of their minds and that she understood why they both so often said in exactly the same tone of puzzled bewilderment: 'I don't see what you're making such a fuss about.' Of course! And then they wanted to be excessively modern, and then they'd think: 'After all, we're in Paris.'

There they were. And there Marya was; haggard, tortured by jealousy, burnt up by longing.

They reached Brunoy. The cab was there and Lois said, exactly as Marya had known she would say: 'I must stop on the way because there's not much to eat in the house.'

The old horse set off at a jog-trot up the street and stopped outside the grocer's shop with its display of piles of dried fruit, packets of coffee and a jovial advertisement for Pâtés de la Lune. Next door, in the hairdresser's window, was the bust of a pink and white lady in a provocative attitude and a huge bottle of bright green liquid; then came a shoemaker's necklaces of hobnailed boots.

It was all very peaceful.

Lois came out, accompanied by a boy carrying parcels; the cabman flicked up his horse; they passed the last houses and the road stretched long and grey in front of them. Marya sat squeezed between the Heidlers, listening to the melancholy sound of the hoofs and the rattling of the old cab. In the dusk the trunks of the trees gleamed as though they were made of some dull metal, but when they had been driving for half an hour it had grown dark and she could only see the shadows of the branches running along in front of the cab. There were lights in the windows of a straggling row of small houses.

The cab stopped. They got out, walked along a muddy path, and Lois pushed a door open and led the way into a room with gay check curtains, straw armchairs, and a divan with coloured cushions. The table was laid ready for a meal.

'D'you want to go up?' asked Lois. 'Here's a candle for you. You know where your room is?'

Marya said that she remembered. She went through the kitchen, up a narrow staircase into a room which smelt sweet and cool. Rabbits chased each other over the wall-paper. The window was wide open and the stillness out-side seemed wonderful after the shriek of Paris. Soft, like velvet.

'Hurry up,' called Lois from the foot of the stairs. 'H. J.'s mixing the cocktails.'

Marya thought: 'Oh, Lord! what a fool I am.' Her heart felt as if it were being pinched between somebody's fingers. Cocktails, the ridiculous rabbits on the wallpaper. All the fun and sweetness of life hurt so abominably when it was always just out of your reach.

Dinner was a silent, solemn meal. A dog howled with melancholy persistency. Lois sat with an invulnerable expression on her dark face. It was as if she were saying: 'You can't down me. My roots go very deep.' She ate heartily and rather noisily, drank a good deal more than usual, and then announced that she was going to bed.

'Goodnight, you two.'

The door shut sharply behind her.

*

'You're not going,' said Heidler to Marya. He came over to take her in his arms.

'You must be mad,' she told him fiercely. 'D'you think I am a *bonne* or something to be made love to every time the mistress's back is turned? Can't you see? You must be the cruellest devil in the world.' She burst into miserable tears.

'I'm as unhappy as you are,' muttered Heidler. His face looked white and lined. He began to argue: 'I don't show it as much as you do, because I've trained myself not to show things, but I'm so miserable that I wish I were dead. You don't help at all, Mado. You make things worse. I love you; I can't help it. It's not your fault; it's not my fault. I love you; I'm burnt up with it. It's a fact. There it is, nobody's fault. Why can't you just accept it instead of straining against it all the time? You make things so difficult for me and for yourself.'

She asked him if he really imagined she could live there between them. And as she asked it, she thought: 'I wonder how many times I've said that. A vain repetition, that's what it is. A vain repetition.'

'I don't see why not,' he said slowly. 'After all, you're supreme here; you've only to say what you want and it will be done.'

There was a loud bump from upstairs. Heidler remarked indifferently:

'There's Lois falling about.'

'Oh, you must go up,' said Marya in a very low voice. 'She may be ill—'

'I'm going,' he answered wearily, taking one of the lamps.

He was away for quite a long time, and she waited with her head in her hands, listening.

Steps, more bumps, the dog in the garden of the next cottage still howling. Then Heidler tramped down the creaking stairs again, the lamp with the green and yellow check shade in his hand.

'Poor Lois is quite seedy,' he remarked, putting the lamp down on the table with an expressionless face. 'She's been awfully sick, nearly fainted.'

Marya asked, without lifting her eyes: 'What's the matter?'

'Well,' said Heidler, 'she thinks it's the cassoulet. So do I. I don't trust this tinned stuff.'

Of course, there they were: inscrutable people, invulnerable people, and she simply hadn't a chance against them, naïve sinner that she was.

*

The night before they were to return to Paris she woke about midnight to a feeling of solitude and desolation. She had gone with Lois down to the village to buy plants, and they had walked almost all the way in dead silence. It was comical, of course, and degrading. They were like two members of a harem who didn't get on. When Lois did speak to her it was with a strained politeness which at moments was cringing – as if she said: I must keep her in a good temper. Marya was brooding, nervous, waiting and hoping for the violent reaction that might free her from an impossible situation.

The room was full of night noises. 'After all,' she thought, 'I can't lie here for ever listening to these cracks and tappings.' She got up, lit the lamp and went downstairs for a bottle of Vittel and a book. There was a light under the sitting-room door. Voices. A vague murmur from Heidler. And then Lois, very clear and loud:

'And she's so rude sometimes – surly. It gets on my nerves. Her whole attitude gets on my nerves. I don't trust her, let me tell you that. She isn't to be trusted.'

Another murmur from Heidler.

'They're talking about me,' Marya told herself. 'They're sitting there talking about me. Those two. I can't stick this,' she thought. 'Not a minute longer. It's got to finish, quick.'

Then she realized that she was holding the lamp at a dangerous angle and put it down on the kitchen table. But her breath had gone. One moment to fill her lungs – she didn't want to stammer stupidly – then she opened the door as noisily as she could.

'Hullo!' said Heidler, looking round.

Lois made a wincing movement with her mouth and pulled her dressing-gown together at the throat, looking frightened.

Marya told them: 'I heard what you said just now.'

'Well, why not?' said Heidler with an expression of good-natured sarcasm.

'You were talking about me.'

'Well,' he asked again, 'and why shouldn't we?'

'You mustn't think. . . .' Her breath had gone again and her voice trembled. 'You mustn't think that I don't realize . . . that I haven't realized for a long time the arrangement that you and Lois have made about me.'

'You're mad,' said Lois with indignation.

'You have made an arrangement!' said Marya loudly. 'Not in so many words, perhaps, a tacit arrangement. If he wants the woman let him have her. Yes. D'you think I don't know?'

Heidler got up and said nervously: 'Don't shout. You can hear every single word that's said at Madame Guyot's next door!'

'*Tant mieux!*' screamed Marya. '*Tant mieux, tant mieux!*'

Lois made a nervous movement.

'No, let me talk to her,' said Heidler. 'You don't understand how to deal with this sort of woman; I do.'

It was horrible, the power he had to hurt her.

'Look out, Heidler,' she said.

'Don't be hysterical,' he told her with contempt, 'talk calmly. What do you want? What's it all about?'

But every vestige of coherence, of reason had fled from her brain. Besides, however reasonably or coherently she talked, they wouldn't understand, either of them. If she said: 'You're torturing me, you're mocking me, you're driving me mad,' they wouldn't understand.

She muttered: 'I'm not going to live with Lois and you any longer. I – am – not! And you must arrange . . .'

'Ah!' said Heidler, 'it's a question of money. I rather thought that was what you were getting at.'

She jumped forward and hit him as hard as she could.

'Horrible German!' she said absurdly. 'Damned German! *Crapule*!' She stood panting, waiting for him to drop his arm that she might hit again.

'You're quite right,' he muttered, and put his head in his hands. 'You're quite right. Oh God! Oh God!'

Lois went up to him and he lifted his head and looked at her with hatred.

'Leave me alone,' he said. 'I've done with you.'

She began to talk in a caressing voice.

'Damn you, leave me alone!' he shouted, and pushed her so that she staggered back against the wall. Then he buried his face in his arms again and began to sob.

Marya's calm came back to her as theirs disappeared. She began to think how ridiculous it all was, that it was chilly, that she wanted to go upstairs, that she had only imagined the love and hate she felt for these two, that she had only imagined that such emotions as love and hate existed at all. She stood looking at the floor, feeling undecided and self-conscious. Then:

'I'm awfully drunk,' said Heidler suddenly, in a calm and as it were explanatory way. 'I'm going to bed. I shan't remember a thing about all this tomorrow morning.'

'He always does that,' Lois remarked in a sisterly manner when he had gone. The contempt had left her voice. It was as if she respected the outburst which seemed to Marya more and more ridiculous and inexcusable.

'When there's been a scene he always says, next morning, that he was drunk and that he doesn't remember anything that happened. It's his way of getting out of things. . . . Why did you come downstairs?'

'I was thirsty.'

'Oh, were you?' Lois said. 'I'll bring you up a bottle of Vittel.'

Marya stared at her, answered with the uttermost politeness: 'No, please don't bother,' and left her anxiously picking up the chair that had fallen down.

*

When she woke next morning the whole thing seemed very unreal and impossible. But even while it was going on it had seemed unreal. She had felt like a marionette, as though something outside her were jerking strings that forced her to scream and strike. Heidler, weeping, was a marionette, too. And Lois, anxious-eyed, in her purple dressing-gown. 'Anyhow,' thought Marya, 'I'm going away. I'll stick to that.'

Peace, the normal, reigned downstairs. Madame Guillot was in the kitchen, bustling about and singing.

'*Bonjour, mademoiselle,*' said Madame Guillot, smiling. '*Pardon. Madame.*'

Twenty years ago Madame Guillot's husband had killed her lover – or the other way round. In any case there had been a tragedy and a scandal, and things had apparently been made pretty hot for Madame Guillot by the village in general. But now here she was singing away among her pots and pans, and her fat back seemed to say: 'Life has got to be lived, mademoiselle or madame. One might as well be cheerful about it.' It was a lovely blue day, too.

'Good morning, my dear,' said Heidler. 'The fly will be here at eleven. I'm coming with you to Paris to help you to find an hotel.'

He looked so calm that their dispute seemed more incredible than ever.

'Lois has gone to the village to shop. She wants to stay on here for a few days and I shall probably come straight back. About money. Well, we'll talk that over at lunch.'

She flushed and turned her head away.

'Look here, H. J. . . .'

'I'm not going to discuss last night,' interrupted Heidler. 'If you're not happy here we must find you an hotel, that's all. But I don't intend to let you go. Don't you make any mistake about that. Of course, if you force me to break with Lois I will. Is that what you're trying to do?'

'No,' she said. 'No. You don't understand me. I'm not trying to force you to do anything.'

He repeated: 'I'll break with her and take you away somewhere. Is that what you want?'

'No, not for anything,' said Marya again. 'No, I can't do that.' She added in a very low voice: 'Be kind to Lois, H. J.'

'Ah?' remarked Heidler. 'H-m!'

He looked half contemptuous, half pitiful, as if he were thinking: 'No, she can't play this game.'

Marya went on sullenly: 'But I couldn't help last night. I couldn't stick it any longer.'

'I'm not saying,' he told her, with a judicial expression, 'that I don't see your point of view.'

She said: 'Why did you say such a damnable thing to me last night? About money.'

'I don't remember saying anything about it,' he answered. 'I remember that you were rather damnable.'

He was still looking steadily at her. His eyes were clear,

cool and hard, but something in the depths of them flickered and shifted. She thought: 'He'd take any advantage he could – fair or unfair. Caddish he is.' Then as she stared back at him she felt a great longing to put her head on his knees and shut her eyes. To stop thinking. Stop the little wheels in her head that worked incessantly. To give in and have a little peace. The unutterably sweet peace of giving in.

She pressed her lips together and said: 'Well, you did. And I hit you. And I'm jolly glad I hit you, too. Look here, I must go and pack.'

'Lois will come up and help you,' said Heidler. 'Yes. I remember your hitting me – quite well.'

When Lois appeared she said, in an oddly apologetic manner: 'You know, Mado, you can't think how sorry I am about all this. What an awful pity I think it is.'

'It doesn't matter,' answered Marya coldly. She hated Lois. She hated her air of guilt. She hated her eyes of a well-trained domestic animal.

Lois continued, with suspicion: 'You are not going to talk to anybody in Paris about all this, are you?'

'Who could I talk to?' asked Marya in an aggressive voice.

But in the cab she said to Heidler over and over again: 'Oh, Heidler, be good to Lois, be good to Lois, you must be good to Lois.'

'I shouldn't worry too much about Lois if I were you,' Heidler answered.

15

CROWDS OF PEOPLE were waiting at the Porte d'Orléans for the trams to Fresnes. They stood with phlegmatic patience, craning their necks, and each tram was immediately packed when it did come with parties going to spend Sunday in the country. With each party was a jocular young man and two girls who giggled, or that was what it seemed like to Marya. The neat little houses slipped past and the endless row of sycamore trees. At the Café of the Cadran Bleu she got down.

The warder who took the permits knew her. His 'Qui êtes-vous?' was mechanical.

'Sa femme.'

'Passez,' said the warder. And she passed into the cobblestoned courtyard. She had begun to have a dreadful feeling of familiarity with the place: the whitewashed corridor that smelt of damp and rot, the stone staircase, the queue of women awaiting their turn in the cubicles. That day it was all arm-in-arm as it were. The drably terrible life of the under-dog.

The prison was familiar, but it seemed to her that Stephan was a stranger: dark-bearded, shaven-headed, very thin, very bright-eyed. He wore – as usual – a piece of sacking over his head and he gripped the bars and leaned forward, talking slowly in his rusty voice.

He asked her why she had left the Heidlers.

'Because you weren't free there? *Mais, tu es folle, Mado.* What do you want to be free for? Have you got a job? What are you going to do now? Really you must be mad to do a thing like that.'

She reminded him, feeling nervous and awkward, that he would be at liberty in four months.

'Only four months! Only four months! My God, it's so easy to talk, isn't it?' He went on irritably, but always with those imploring eyes of a small boy. 'How do I know what will happen when I am free? I've no money. I'll have to leave France. You have friends and you lose them. You're not clever. But I don't mean to quarrel. I'm going off my head here. You're not vexed?'

'No,' she said. 'No, no, no.'

'Last Sunday,' he said, 'when you didn't come I felt awful. Of course, I didn't get your letter in time and I was waiting for them to call out my number when visiting-time came. Every number that was called out I thought was mine. And it never was. And then I thought, "She's late today." And then I thought, "She's never as late as this. She must be ill. She's not coming." But still I couldn't help listening for my number each time they called. I was glad when the time was up, I can tell you. It sounds nothing, but it was awful. One goes mad shut up here.'

She smiled. 'I never will not turn up again, Stephan. Never. So don't worry.'

The warder banged open the door and snarled. Stephan disappeared.

As she walked away she knew why the prison had seemed closer and more terrible than ever before. It was because the thought of Heidler had always stood between her and the horror of it. He was big and calm and comforting. He said: 'Don't worry. I love you, d'you see?' And one hadn't worried. At least, not so much.

She sat in the corner of the tram watching the sycamore trees speed past.

Heidler, Heidler, Heidler.

Supposing she asked him, next time she saw him: 'Heidler, save me. I'm afraid. Save me.' Just like that. Then he'd think her a coward. 'I wonder if I am a coward,' reflected Marya. And then: 'And how many of them could stick it – all the people who'd call me coward? Not many – with their well-fed eyes and their long upper lips.' Something hard and dry in her chest was hurting her.

When she got back to her hotel, which was near the Gare de Montparnasse, she took all Heidler's letters and re-read them. Five letters. She had left Brunoy four days before. Very good letters they were, too. Very convincing. She had answered once – shortly and coldly. The fifth and last letter told her that he was coming to the Hôtel du Bosphore to see her the next afternoon. It began: 'Dearest. Dearest in all the world,' and ended with an effect as of a sudden attack of caution – 'So I'll be with you about four. Yours H.'

*

The Hôtel du Bosphore looked down on Montparnasse station, where all day a succession of shabby trains, each trailing its long scarf of smoke, clanked slowly backwards and forwards.

Behind the trains a background of huge advertisements: A scarlet haired baby Cadum: a horrible little boy in a sailor suit: *Exigez toujours du Lion Noir.* A horrible little girl with a pigtail: *Evitez le contrefaçons.*

An atmosphere of departed and ephemeral loves hung about the bedroom like stale scent, for the hotel was one of unlimited hospitality, though quietly, discreetly and not more so than most of its neighbours. The wallpaper was vaguely erotic – huge and fantastically shaped mauve, green and yellow flowers sprawling on a black ground. There was one chair and a huge bed covered with a pink counterpane. It was impossible, when one looked at that bed, not to think of the succession of *petites femmes* who had extended themselves upon it, clad in carefully thought out pink or mauve chemises, full of tact and savoir faire and savoir vivre and all the rest of it.

On the morning after her visit to Fresnes, Marya woke early and dressed slowly, listening for the man with the flock of goats who passed under her window every morning at about half-past ten, playing a frail little tune on a pipe. He was a sturdy man who looked as if he were out in all weathers. He wore country clothes and a *béret basque*, and he carried on his back a black bag marked in white letters: *Fromage de chèvre.*

But it was the little tune he played which enchanted her. Not a gay blast on a trumpet like the glazier. He also passed, but earlier. This was thin, high, sweet music like water running in the sun, and the man played, not to attract customers, but to keep his flock in order. They were wonderful goats, five of them, all black and white, and they crossed the street calmly, avoiding trams with dignity and skill. One behind the other and no jostling, like the perfect ladies that they were.

Marya listened to the music of the pipe, dwindling away in the distance, persistent as the hope of happiness. Then she lunched at Boots' Bar (once A la Savoyard, renamed by the proprietor, an anglophile), and after lunch went back to her melancholy bedroom and slept, for she had lain awake all night, tormented by doubts and fears. When she awoke, bewildered, Heidler was there looking down on her.

She had meant to tell him: 'I love you. You aren't making any mistake about that, are you?' But all she said was: 'Please will you draw the curtains?'

'H. J. . . .'

'What is it, my darling?'

'You aren't sad?'

'My dear, no, of course not.'

She said: 'Listen. I feel as if I'd fallen down a precipice.'

'You funny thing,' said Heidler.

But that was how she felt. Because she knew that she would never be able even to pretend to fight him again, and because, when she looked anxiously into his eyes, she had imagined that they were sad and cold like ashes.

'Well, look here, my dear one, I must go. I've got to—' He stopped.

Of course he'd been going to say, 'I've got to go back to Lois.'

She thought: 'I must get used to this. No use making a fuss,' and fixed a mechanical smile on her lips.

'Don't get up,' said Heidler. 'I'll send you in dinner and some wine. And a book. Have you got any books? It's horrible outside.'

When he went he left the door open. The gramophone belonging to the South American gentleman next door was playing 'I want to be happy.' Naturally.

*

He was very different next morning. A new Heidler, one she had never seen before. To begin with, he wore a bowler hat. When they were seated in the Restaurant de Versailles she was still thinking uneasily about the hat, because it seemed symbolical of a new attitude. He looked self-possessed, respectable, yet not without a certain hard rakishness. There is something impressive, something which touches the imagination about the sight of an English bowler hat in the Rue de Rennes. . . . In the middle of the meal he announced:

'Lois is expecting you to tea this afternoon.'

'But I don't want to go.'

'My darling child,' said Heidler with calmness, 'your whole point of view and your whole attitude to life is impossible and wrong and you've got to change it for everybody's sake.'

He went on to explain that one had to keep up appearances. That everybody had to. Everybody had for everybody's sake to keep up appearances. It was everybody's duty, it was in fact what they were there for.

'You've got to play the game.'

Marya said: 'Lois simply wants me around so that she can tear me to bits and get her friends to help her to tear me to bits.' She added slowly: 'They'll tear me up and show you the bits. That's what will happen. And you won't see it. A Frenchman would see the game at once, but you won't see it, or you pretend not to.'

'Rubbish!' said Heidler, looking vexed. 'Lois is very fond of you. One's got to take certain things into account which may not seem to you very important. But which . . .' His nose seemed to lengthen oddly as he spoke.

Marya thought: 'He looks exactly like a picture of Queen Victoria.'

But he was convincing, impressive and full of authority. He overwhelmed her. She made one last effort.

'H.J., Lois doesn't like me,' she said. 'She can't possibly want to see me.'

'I tell you that she's extremely fond of you,' asserted Heidler. 'She's always saying so. She's very sorry for you, for the dreadful life you've had and all that.'

'Ah,' said Marya, helplessly.

'I hate explaining these things,' Heidler went on fretfully. 'I hate talking about things, but you surely must see that you can't let Lois down. Everybody knows that you were staying with us and if there's a definite split it will give the whole show away. I can't let Lois down,' he kept saying, 'we must keep up appearances, we must play the game.'

Marya told him at last miserably: 'Oh, all right, of course.'

'Savage,' he said, watching her, 'Bolshevist! You'll end up in red Russia, that's what will happen to you.'

'I thought that you understood that in me.'

'Oh, theoretically,' answered Heidler. 'Theoretically, of course I do. My darling, have a chartreuse and don't look so miserable.'

'But he really is like Queen Victoria sometimes,' thought Marya.

He took his bowler hat and they departed. They bought cakes on the way.

Lois greeted Marya in a high voice and with a gleam of triumph in her eyes. She wore a gown of purple georgette, silk stockings and high-heeled shoes. She had changed the colour of her face-powder and looked younger. Below the décolleté of her dress was a glimpse of a rose-coloured chemise.

Marya thought: 'How ridiculous we both are,' and sat on the divan feeling like a captive attached to somebody's chariot wheels.

Miss Nicholson arrived, and Mrs O'Mara, and the Satterbys and Guy and partner, and several young men of various nationalities.

Lois handed cups of tea and ordered Heidler about and called Marya 'Darling Mado' when he was there, and was spiteful when he was out of earshot. They talked about a new dance club they were starting, and whether the Countess Stadkioff ought to be barred.

'Bar a countess?' Marya expected to hear Lois say. 'No, certainly not.' She turned politely in her direction. But, to her surprise, Lois nodded.

Everybody said: 'Yes, we'll bar the countess this time.' Then they all looked relieved, as though they had sacrificed to some tribal god.

Miss Anna Nicholson, who painted landscapes and was a very bright talker indeed, was witty about the colour of the countess's hair.

She was Lois's friend and confidante and, as she talked,

115

she watched Marya with amused and virginal eyes. She was thinking:

'The idea of a woman making such an utter fool of herself. It's hardly to be believed. Her hand is trembling. No poise. . . . Lois needn't be afraid of her. But then, Lois is a bit of a fool herself. Englishwomen very often are.'

16

THE LITTLE CLOCK on the table by the bed was ticking so loudly that Marya got up and shut it away in a drawer. But she could still hear it, fussy and persistent. Then a train gave a long piercing shriek and she sighed, turned on the light and lay contemplating the flowers which crawled like spiders over the black walls of her bedroom. The mechanism of her brain got to work with a painful jerk and began to tick in time with the clock.

She made a great effort to stop it and was able to keep her mind a blank for, say, ten seconds. Then her obsession gripped her, arid, torturing, gigantic, possessing her as utterly as the longing for water possesses someone who is dying of thirst. She had made an utter mess of her love affair, and that was that. She had made an utter mess of her existence. And that was that, too.

But of course it wasn't a love affair. It was a fight. A ruthless, merciless, three-cornered fight. And from the first Marya, as was right and proper, had no chance of victory. For she fought wildly, with tears, with futile rages, with extravagant abandon — all bad weapons.

'What's the matter with you?' she would ask herself. 'Why are you like this? Why can't you be clever? Pull yourself together!' Uselessly.

'No self-control,' thought Marya. 'That's what's the matter with me. No training.'

But of course he was very clever. And Lois, just sitting tight and smiling, was very clever. Oh, very clever! And she, Marya, was a fool who could do nothing but cry behind a locked door.

She shut her eyes and at once his face was close to hers, hard and self-contained. 'All that!' his cool eyes said. 'Oh, yes, very nice. But all that grows on every blackberry bush, my dear.' His cool eyes that confused and hurt her.

He wasn't a good lover, of course. He didn't really like women. She had known that as soon as he touched her. His hands were inexpert, clumsy at caresses; his mouth was hard when he kissed. No, not a lover of women, he could say what he liked.

He despised love. He thought of it grossly, to amuse himself, and then with ferocious contempt. Not that that mattered. He might be right. On the other hand, he might just possibly be wrong. But it didn't really matter much.

What mattered was that, despising, almost disliking, love, he was forcing her to be nothing but the little woman who lived in the Hôtel du Bosphore for the express purpose of being made love to. A *petite femme*. It was, of course, part of his mania for classification. But he did it with such conviction that she, miserable weakling that she was, found herself trying to live up to his idea of her.

She lived up to it. And she had her reward.

'. . . You pretty thing – you pretty, pretty thing. Oh, you darling. I say, did you notice what I did with my wrist-watch? Lois has got hold of two Czecho-Slovakians and that young American chap – you know – what's-his-name? – the sculptor – for tonight and I promised I'd turn up. Are you all right for money? I'd better leave some money, hadn't I?'

The endless repetition of that sort of thing became a torture. She would wait for him to say, 'Look here, I must go now. Because Lois . . .'

As he dressed she would lie with one arm over her eyes and think: 'A bedroom in hell might look rather like this one. Yellow-green and dullish mauve flowers crawling over black walls.'

Her lips were dry. Her body ached. He was so heavy. He crushed her. He bore her down.

The dim room smelt of stale scent. She began to imagine all the women who had lain where she was lying. Laughing. Or crying if they were drunk enough. She felt giddy and curiously light, as if she were floating about bodiless in the scented dimness.

'It's frightfully hot in here,' Heidler was saying. 'D'you mind if I pull the curtains and open the window? Where's your handbag? Look here – do go and dine somewhere decent, for God's sake.'

He always hurried the end of his dressing, as if getting out of her bedroom would be an escape.

'Yes,' said Marya dully. 'All right. I will.'

'It oughtn't to be like this. I oughtn't to let it be like this. It's ugly like this.'

All very well to think that. But he crushed her. He bore her down.

Besides, she hadn't a leg to stand on, really. He had everything on his side – right down to the expression on the waiter's face when he brought up her breakfast. Everything. Including Logic and Common Sense. For he could so easily say – he often did say – 'Why did you leave the Avenue de l'Observatoire?'

Or, 'Why don't you come along with me and see Lois? Come to Lefranc's tomorrow for lunch. Lois is very fond of you. And you must turn up occasionally, my dear; you really must.'

They would be sitting in the Café de Versailles, a peaceful place at three o'clock in the afternoon, given up to middle-aged gentlemen drinking bocks and young men writing letters. The vague smell of lunch still hung on the air. Outside, the Rue de Rennes stewed drearily in the sun.

'I don't want people to know anything. It isn't anybody's business. We can't let Lois down, surely you must see that. She's been awfully generous and we can't let her down.'

'But everybody knows already,' said Marya. 'If you think they don't, your crest ought to be an ostrich.'

'Nonsense!'

She persisted. 'Everybody cuts me dead all along the Boulevard Montparnasse, anyway. Even De Solla cuts me. I'm the villain of the piece, and they do know. They say that Lois picked me up when I was starving and that the moment I got into her house I tried to get hold of you. And that there are limits. Or they say – shall I tell you what else they say, the ones who have lived here long enough?'

'Oh, I know the sort of thing,' said Heidler. 'But what if they do? They can't be sure. You must live it down. My dear child, you can live everything down, believe me, if you keep your head and don't give yourself away.'

'And if you have a good little income. Don't forget that.'

'Why should I be a butt for Lois and her friends?' Marya went on excitedly. 'She wants me there so that she can talk at me. She wants me there so that she can watch out for the right moment to put her enormous foot down.'

She began to laugh loudly. There was a coarse sound in her laughter. Heidler looked at her sideways. He disliked her when she laughed like that.

He told her coldly: 'You talk the most awful nonsense sometimes, don't you?'

'What?' said Marya. 'Aren't Lois's feet enormous? Well, I think they are. You didn't exactly look for *fines attaches* when you married, did you?'

His eyes were very hostile. When she saw his hostile eyes she stopped laughing and her lips trembled.

'All right. Very well. Just as you like,' said Marya. 'What's it matter, anyway?'

It was no good arguing, there she was, the villain of the piece; and it hurt, of course. When the lonely night came it started hurting like hell. Then she would drink a couple of Pernods at Boots's Bar to deaden the hurt and, carefully avoiding the Boulevard du Montparnasse, she would walk to a side-street off the Boulevard St Michel and dine in a students' restaurant, not frequented by the Montparnos.

'A Pernod fils, please.'

'Pernod is very bad for the stomach, mademoiselle,' the *patronne* said disapprovingly. 'If mademoiselle had a Dubonnet instead?'

The *patronne* was really a wonderfully good sort. Fancy caring what happened to the stomach of a stray client. On the other hand, fancy facing life – that is to say, facing Heidler and Lois – on a Dubonnet! Marya could have cackled with laughter.

'No, a Pernod,' she insisted.

And a minute afterwards the merciful stuff clouded her brain. Then, dazed, she watched the lady who was sitting opposite dining slowly and copiously. Soup; a beefsteak; a salad; cheese. She was a lady with a pale face, crimson lips, a close-fitting black hat, and eyebrows like half moons. She was indeed exactly like Pierrot and every now and then she would turn and look at herself in the glass approvingly. Eventually, gathering up her belongings, she moved out with stately and provocative undulations of the hips.

But the students at the next table were *camelots du roi*. They were talking politics and the lady passed out unnoticed. Then Marya, imitating her, turned round and looked at herself in the mirror at the back, powdered her face and reddened her lips. But hopelessly, thinking, 'Good God, how ugly I've grown!' Loving had done that to her – among other things – made her ugly. If this was love – this perpetual aching longing, this wound that bled persistently and very slowly. And the devouring hope. And the fear. That was the worst. The fear she lived with – that the little she had would be taken from her.

Love was a terrible thing. You poisoned it and stabbed

at it and knocked it down into the mud – well down –
and it got up and staggered on, bleeding and muddy and
awful. Like – like Rasputin. Marya began to laugh.

As she walked back to the hotel after her meal Marya
would have the strange sensation that she was walking under
water. The people passing were like the wavering reflections
seen in water, the sound of water was in her ears. Or
sometimes she would feel sure that her life was a dream –
that all life was a dream. 'It's a dream,' she would think;
'it isn't real' – and be strangely comforted.

A dream. A dream. '*La vie toute faite des morceaux. Sans
suite comme des rêves.*' Who wrote that? Gauguin. '*Sans
suite comme des rêves.*' A dream. Long shining empty streets
and tall dark houses looking down at her.

Often during these walks she passed under the windows
of the studio in the Avenue de l'Observatoire. Once it was
on a Thursday night. Lois's party, of course. She stood outside in the dark street imagining that she heard the sound of
the gramophone playing, 'If you knew Suzie like I know Suzie'.

Then she thought, 'No, this is too stupid. I'm going
home.' But still she stood there listening, looking up at
the lit windows.

Well, there she was In a bad way. Hard hit. All in. And
a drunkard into the bargain. And she had to stuff herself
with veronal before she could sleep.

But when she tried to argue reasonably with herself it
seemed to her that she had forgotten the beginnings of the
affair, when she had still reacted and he had reconquered
her painstakingly. She never reacted now. She was a
thing. Quite dead. Not a kick left in her.

When Lois sneered she sat with bent head and never answered.

'Oh, I know I've got a terrible tongue,' Lois would say complacently. And Marya, watching her, silent, would think: 'One of these days just when she's thought of something clever to say about me for her friends to snigger at, just when she's opening her mouth to say it, I'll smash a wine-bottle in her face.'

Sitting there silent, her hands cold and a little fixed smile on her face, she would imagine the sound of the glass breaking, the sight of the blood streaming. As she lay awake she imagined it, breathing quickly, and then she would tell herself, horrified: 'My God, I'm going mad!'

Little wheels in her head that turned perpetually. I love him. I want him. I hate her. And he's a swine. He's out to hurt me. What shall I do? I love him. I want him. I hate her.

So she would lie for hours, tortured by love and hate, till the morning came and the coloured tepid water which they called coffee in the Hôtel du Bosphore. Then she would get up and look at herself in the glass, thinking: 'Good Lord! can that be me? No wonder people think I'm a bad lot.'

Her eyelids were swollen and flaccid over unnaturally large, bright eyes. Her head seemed to have sunk between her shoulders, giving her a tormented and deformed look. Her mouth drooped, her skin was greyish, and when she made up her face the powder and rouge stood out in clownish patches.

She would stare at herself, feeling a horrible despair.

A feeling of sickness would come over her as she stared at herself. She would get back into bed and lie huddled with her arm over her eyes.

This was Marya's life for six days of the week. On the seventh she went to Fresnes and returned soothed, comforted, and, because she reacted physically so quickly, once more desirable.

'My dear, how much better you look!' Heidler would never fail to remark the next day. 'Not half so peaky. My darling child. You pretty thing.'

Marya thought of her husband with a passion of tenderness and protection. He represented her vanished youth – her youth, her gaiety, her joy in life. She would tell herself: 'He was kind to me. He was awfully chic with me.'

Soon, for her sentimental mechanism was very simple, she extended this passion to all the inmates of the prison, to the women who waited with her under the eye of the fat warder, to all unsuccessful and humbled prostitutes, to everybody who wasn't plump, sleek, satisfied, smiling and hard-eyed. To all the people who never went to tea-parties or gave them. To everybody, in fact, who was utterly unlike the Heidlers.

She went to the prison gaily, as if she were going to visit a friend, and all the way there she would revolve her plans for Stephan.

*

It was the beginning of August. Stephan was to be released on the second Sunday in September.

'I'll have to find a coiffeur,' he said anxiously. 'I don't

125

want to go around Paris with my hair on my shoulders and a long beard. . . .'

The warder who shaved the prisoners' heads was, it seemed, a good sort. A few weeks before they were released he let them start to grow their hair.

'Not a bad type,' said Stephan. 'Many of them are not bad. They do their work, what do you wish? I daresay they'd prefer to do something else.'

'Oh, you'll find a coiffeur,' said Marya. 'I'll get a room for you in the Quartier Latin somewhere, will that do?'

'Look in the Rue Tollman,' he advised.

'Well, you can go straight there from Fresnes and in the afternoon I'll turn up with the money.'

'It's all very well,' said Stephan, 'but what about you? How will you manage about money?'

She answered: 'I've told you, the Heidlers have lent me some money.'

'They're chic,' remarked Stephan.

17

AUGUST WAS A HOT, oppressive month, the sun beating down on sleepy streets, the cafés and restaurants nearly empty, the staircase and passages of the Hôtel du Bosphore and its fellows pervaded by an extraordinary mixture of smells. Drains, face powder, scent, garlic, drains. Above all, drains, Heidler decided. He reached the second floor and knocked at Marya's door.

'I'm not late,' he said when she opened it. 'Your clock's fast.' He sat down, with a sigh, thinking: 'Oh, God, what depressing places hotel bedrooms can be.' He looked at the bed, averted his eyes instantly and lit a cigarette. When he had smoked it, he suggested:

'Why shouldn't you go into the country for a bit? Somewhere not too far from Brunoy. Paris is hateful in August. And you really aren't looking well.'

'I can't go away just now,' she told him. 'What's the good? I must be here when my husband comes out of jail.'

'Oh! Of course,' said Heidler. He coughed and added: 'But look here, my dear, you surely don't intend. . . .'

'Intend what?'

There was an edge to her voice.

'If you go back to your husband,' he declared, 'I can't see you again, you understand that?' He leaned back, looking impenetrable and alert, like a chess-player who has just made a good move.

It was a greyish day and she was sitting with her back to the light. He couldn't see her face well. She answered sharply:

'I'm certainly going to see Stephan and do what I can for him. It won't be much. Are you thinking of trying to stop me, you and your damned Lois?'

She was astonished at herself. 'After all,' she thought, 'I've still got a kick left in me.'

Heidler began to argue patiently, talking as it were from the other side of a gulf between them.

'You don't seem to realize that I'm merely trying to save you from a very dreadful existence, an unthinkable existence. Your husband is going to be expelled from France. And he's in trouble with the Belgian police, you say. Have you imagined what your life will be? You'll career about Europe without any money or any friends in a perpetual and horrible insecurity. And sooner or later he'll probably try to get back to Paris. That's what they all do, it seems. They come back to Paris and hide till they're arrested again. I mean, I'm not going to be mixed up with all that sort of thing. I can't be. I can't afford to be. You simply don't know what you're letting yourself in for, my dear. I'm trying to stop you from having anything to do with him for your own sake.'

'I shall never live with him again. That's finished,' said Marya.

'Oh!' answered Heidler. 'That's all right then.'

She went on: 'But d'you think I could possibly be more miserable than I have been during the last few months? How could I? Don't you understand that I'm unbearably miserable?'

'No,' he answered, still patiently. 'I'm afraid that I don't understand – I do my best.'

'Oh, don't you? Don't you?' She was excited and bitter. 'Don't you understand that I hate this *louche* hotel and the bedroom and the wallpaper and the whole situation, and my whole life?'

'Why don't you change your hotel?'

'All these sort of hotels are the same,' she said drearily. 'It's the whole situation, I tell you. It's my own fault. I've been a fool. I've let Lois—'

'Why not leave Lois out of the question? She has nothing to do with it. She had nothing to do with it.'

'Oh, one word to that,' said Marya rudely. 'She had a lot to do with it, and you know it. You drink in every word she says about me.'

'You imagine that.' He looked at his watch and sighed.

'You've smashed me up, you two,' she was saying.

That was pitiful because it was so obviously true. It was also in an obscure way rather flattering.

She put her hands up to her face and began to cry. Long-fingered hands she had with very beautifully shaped nails. She cried quietly, all soft and quivering, her little breasts heaving up and down in painful, regular jerks.

'I'm still fond of her,' he told himself. 'If only she'd leave it at that.'

But no. She took her hands away from her face and started to talk again. What a bore! Now, of course, she was quite incoherent.

'The most utter nonsense,' thought Heidler. Utter nonsense about (of all things) the visiting cards stuck into the looking-glass over Lois's damned mantelpiece, about

Lois's damned smug pictures and Lois's damned smug voice. She said that Lois and he pretended to be fair and were hard as hell underneath. She said they couldn't feel anything and pretended that nobody else could. She said that she hated their friends.

'Imagining they know a thing when they know its name,' said Marya. 'And guzzling and yapping at Lefranc's.'

Heidler was stung and interrupted coldly:

'It's extraordinary that you don't see how unintelligent it is of you to abuse Lois.'

But she didn't take the slightest notice. She just went on talking. She drank so much that she was getting as hoarse as a crow. He tried not to listen. He wouldn't listen to this torrent of nonsense. Then he heard her say in a cold hard voice:

'Didn't you say that sex was a ferocious thing?'

He answered: 'Oh yes. So it is. A terrible thing. I ought to know that.'

He was still watching the shape of her breasts under the thin silk dress she wore – a dark-coloured, closely fitting dress that suited her.

'Terrible as an army set in array. Terrible and pitiful and futile,' he thought. 'All that. And a nuisance, too.'

She mocked: 'So it is. So it is. But you don't really believe it, do you? Well, one day I'll walk into your studio and strangle your cad of a Lois – kill her, d'you see? Get my hands round her thick throat and squeeze. Then, perhaps, you'll believe it.'

He said calmly: 'I know. As a matter of fact, I've thought several times that you might try some nonsense of that sort. So has she. So I'll simply give the concierge orders not to let you up in future if you do come. I'm not going to have Lois threatened, don't you make any mistake.'

'Oh, H. J.,' she said. 'Oh, H. J.,' in a little voice like a child.

In the shadow he saw her face crimson and then go white. He got up then because she was so white and trembling and took her in his arms and said pityingly:

'There! There! There!'

When he kissed her her lips were cold.

He said again: 'There! There! There!' And took two clumsy steps forwards, still holding her. She collapsed on to the bed and lay there breathing loudly and quickly as if she had been running. He stood looking down on her, feeling helpless and rather alarmed. He knelt down and stared at her. Her head had dropped backwards over the edge of the bed and from that angle her face seemed strange to him: the cheek-bones looked higher and more prominent, the nostrils wider, the lips thicker. A strange little Kalmuck face.

He whispered: 'Open your eyes, savage. Open your eyes, savage.'

She opened her eyes and said: 'I love you, I love you, I love you. Oh, please be nice to me. Oh, please say something nice to me. I love you.'

She was quivering and abject in his arms, like some unfortunate dog abasing itself before its master.

They dined at a restaurant on the other side of the river, and he felt tender towards her and very anxious to see her smile and be happy. He began to talk about the studio he was going to take on the Boulevard Raspail and the way they were planning to decorate it.

Then: 'I suppose that will get on her nerves, too,' he thought. And stopped abruptly.

She was tired, unable to respond to his gentleness as eagerly as usual.

While they were drinking coffee she said suddenly: 'I'm going to see Stephan, you know.'

'Of course,' agreed Heidler. 'I quite understand that you want to help him. I meant that your going back to live with him would make an impossible situation.'

The next time he saw her he suggested a meeting with Stephan in the Taverne du Panthéon, and Marya lost herself in wonder at this suggestion. Was it his idea of playing the game? Or was Lois curious? Probably it was that, she decided.

18

'MONSIEUR HAS ARRIVED,' announced the landlady of
the hotel in the Rue Tollman 'Yes. Number 19, Madame,
the room you booked.'

When Marya opened the door of Room 19 Stephan was
sitting at the table writing a letter. He looked like some
frail and shrunken apostle, his beard and hair flowed.

When he took her in his arms she felt his thin body
tremble. It was as if a stranger were touching her.

She said: 'Hello, my dear. Well, couldn't you find a
coiffeur's shop open after all?'

He explained that he had been kept at the Palais de
Justice for several hours. 'And I wanted to be here when
you came. Oh, I know that I look awful.'

She smiled at him and answered: 'You look a regular
Montparno.' – 'I didn't know how thin he was,' she was
thinking.

'There's a place open just round the corner. I'll go there
now,' said Stephan.

She walked restlessly up and down the room till he
came back shaved and carrying a cardboard box of cream
cakes. As he opened the box, she watched his hands: thin,
brown, quickly moving. Clever hands he had.

'A savarin, an éclair, two meringues – the ones you
like, and I've ordered tea downstairs. I looked for flowers
but I didn't see any.'

'But I can't eat all those cakes,' she told him.

'Well, you must. You don't look well, Mado. You look – I don't know; you're changed. Oh, zut!' He lit a cigarette. 'Don't let's be sad.'

'No, don't let's be sad,' she said and thought again: 'He's simply dreadfully thin.' Every bone in his face showed. His clothes hung on him.

The tea arrived.

'Arrange yourself on the bed, Mado. It's more comfortable.' He piled pillows behind her back, poured the tea out and brought the cup, waiting on her with anxious gentleness.

She ate and drank quickly and then lay back, relaxed. Gradually an irrational feeling of security and happiness took possession of her. She sighed deeply like a child when a fit of crying is over, lit a cigarette and smoked it slowly, luxuriously. It was extraordinary, but there it was. This was the only human being with whom she had ever felt safe or happy.

His old grey felt hat was lying at the foot of the bed.

She said: 'About your clothes – I packed them all away in your trunk. They're at the Hôtel de l'Univers.'

'Oh, I'll sell the lot,' answered Stephan. 'The less I have with me the better.'

A shaft of sunlight made patterns through the lace curtains on the carpet. It was oppressively hot and airless in the little bedroom. From some distant – probably subterranean – region came the sound of a laboriously played piano.

She opened her handbag and looked at herself in the little glass, and was astounded because her mouth was so smiling and peaceful.

Stephan, seated in the one armchair near the window, was saying: 'I'll be able to stay four days in Paris. A type who left Fresnes with me this morning is going to lend me some money tomorrow. And with what you've brought . . . You know, I took care of the books at the end – the library – oh, my dear, *what* a selection of books! I'll tell you that one day. Well, this man, a Russian Jew, Schlamovitz is his name, was there, too. We talked sometimes – it was a funny life – well, if you knew.' He was silent, as if he were remembering the bizarre and cynical conversations of the Santé and Fresnes. 'He lives with a girl in Montmartre and she was there to meet him this morning.'

'What sort of girl?' asked Marya, interested.

'Oh, well, a *grue*, it seems. But she's a good girl. She was awfully happy when she saw him.'

'Was she?'

'Yes. She cried. Oh, they're fond of their men, these girls, I tell you.'

Marya looked away. But there had been no reproach in his voice, and he went on speaking very quickly and excitedly about the man Schlamovitz who, it seemed, spent an extraordinary existence, being petted by women in Montmartre ('My dear, what a beautiful boy!') and at regular intervals being arrested and taken to jail. He had been expelled from Paris two years before.

'Well,' said Stephan. 'What can you expect? When he was fourteen a rich old woman adopted him. And she made love to him very soon because he was so beautiful. Then she died without leaving him a penny.'

There was also another individual released two days before, known as Michel the nigger, a former soldier of the Foreign Legion, who would put a knife in anybody's back as soon as look at him. 'But a *bon camarade*.' Michel was apparently contemplating reform and turning an honest sou or two. He had a soap-making apparatus in his little two-roomed flat.

'Yes. That transparent soap, you know. And he makes cold cream and the stuff women put on their faces at night.'

'Skin food? Good Lord! All that in his two rooms?'

'Yes,' said Stephan. 'Of course, his wife helps him. And he sells it to the big Paris stores very cheap. But it seems that it's awfully cheap to make. The pots are the most expensive part of it.'

Marya considered him all the while he was talking, and thought: 'He's changed, he's awfully changed.'

She said suddenly, 'If anybody tried to catch me and lock me up I'd fight like a wild animal; I'd fight till they let me out or till I died.'

Stephan laughed. 'Oh, no, you wouldn't, not for long, believe me. You'd do as the others do – you'd wait and be a wild animal when you came out.' He put his hand to his eyes and added: 'When you come out – but you don't come out. Nobody ever comes out.'

She stared at him, impressed by this phrase.

'Let's not talk of it. Later on, Marya, one day I'll tell you everything, everything from the beginning, but let it go now for a while, let it . . .' He began to walk up and down the room. 'Imagine. In a few more days, no more Paris for me. I can't believe it.'

'Don't think about it,' she said, 'don't let's think.'

Then he told her that he had determined to go to

Amsterdam, that he knew a man there who might help him, a Jew, a friend of his father's.

'People abuse Jews, but sometimes they help you when nobody else will.'

'Yes,' said Marya, 'I think so, too. They often understand better than other people.'

But now peace had left her again. She was too restless to lie still. She got up and, sitting on the edge of the bed, watched him gesticulate. His optimism seemed pitiful to her, and strange. She remembered Stephan calm, silent and self-contained; now it was as if prison had broken him up.

He assured her that in six weeks' time he would have arranged something and that he would send for her.

'Can you manage for another six weeks?'

'Of course,' muttered Marya. 'I must tell him,' she thought, and then: 'Oh, I can't now — I must wait a bit. It would be too horribly cruel.' She lit a cigarette, let it go out and then tore it to pieces.

'Don't strew tobacco on my bed, Marya,' said Stephan. 'And, look here, I want to be able to thank your friends, the Heidlers. I suppose they can't want to meet me, but all the same I would like to thank them. It was *chic* what they did, to take you into their house when I was in jail and to be your friends; yes, it was *chic*.'

'Wasn't it?' said Marya in a hard voice.

She asked for another cigarette and went on: 'They'll be in the Taverne this evening at half-past nine, if you want to see them. The Panthéon, you know. But why should you want to? Don't let's go.' She thought of Lois's brown eyes raking Stephan, shabby and shrunken, and she repeated: 'Don't let's go.'

'Are you ashamed of me?' he asked. 'Am I such a scarecrow, so *mocho as* all that?'

'Good God, no!' she said. 'You really want to see them? All right.'

'Is Madame Heidler pretty?' inquired Stephan.

'No,' answered Marya. Then she added at once: 'I don't know. She has lovely eyes; she dances well. . . .'

'Good!' said Stephan, '*à la bonheur*! And now, how about two Mominettes in the little bar on the corner?'

*

Almost immediately after they reached the café Marya, who had her eyes fixed on the door, saw Lois come in and look round with an expression of defiance. Heidler followed her. They came up to the table and sat down. The horrible moment of meeting was over.

Lois began a smooth and tactful monologue. As she talked she fidgeted with her long necklace of huge, brownish yellow beads and watched the ex-convict with antagonism and curiosity.

'Oh, is that so, Madame?' from Stephan.

Heidler had carefully arranged his face to look perfectly expressionless, but when he lit a cigarette his hand trembled. He cut Stephan's thanks short with nervousness. Silence. And then more desperate conversation about the café – how old it was, how famous it was, how ugly it was.

Marya gazed intently at a woman behind the counter and wondered whether she wore a wig or whether her hair had by some extraordinary freak of nature remained blonde, supple, and vital above her rather terrible mask of an avaricious and sensual old woman.

'If it's a wig,' thought Marya, 'it's the most marvellous one I've ever seen. It's darker at the roots. Can't be a wig.'

She stared at the woman, who was arranging a huge green bow round the neck of a minute and hairy dog that stood on the counter, shivering violently. Then she listened again to the careful and nervous conversation of her three companions, and every time she heard Lois's sharply patronizing accents a feeling of such intense irritation shot through her that she clenched her hands under the table.

'For God's sake,' she said suddenly, 'ask the waiter for a *fine*; I'm so thirsty.'

Stephan began to protest. 'Don't have brandy, Mado. She oughtn't to drink brandy, you know . . .' Heidler gave him a furious glance; Lois lifted her eyebrows.

'*Garçon, une fine pour Madame.*'

Another silence.

The violin wailed with pathos: 'Laugh, Pagliacci, for your love is ended.'

Three girls passed the table, disappeared into a door marked telephone and emerged shortly afterwards, relieved, powdered and smiling, their lips very red. The woman behind the counter kissed her dog passionately, calling it the *fille de sa mémère*.

Lois looked round her in an undecided fashion, fixed her eyes on a wall painting and murmured: 'Well, I'm afraid. . . .'

'You're coming back with us, aren't you?' said Heidler to Marya with authority. 'We'll drop you at your hotel.'

She looked at Stephan. He made a quick movement:

'You're very kind, Monsieur,' he said; 'I'll take her home.'

'Oh, I think she'd better come with us,' answered Heidler, staring over Stephan's head. 'It's all on the way.'

'And it's pouring with rain,' added Lois.

'I'll meet you at the little restaurant near the Panthéon tomorrow, Stephan,' said Marya without looking at him.

The three got up. The violin was still wailing. Stephan bowed. Heidler muttered something, looking rather awkward. At the door, she looked back and saw her husband leaning forward staring after them.

*

'Well, he looks all right,' said Lois in the taxi. She spoke with cool contempt. 'And his hair's not short, that's one good thing for him, isn't it?'

'No, on the contrary, it was too long,' Marya told her.

'I think he seems quite all right,' continued Lois. 'I shouldn't worry about him at all, if I were you.'

Marya stared at her without answering.

As they passed Montparnasse station: 'Stop here, will you,' she said. 'I want to get a taxi.'

'What d'you want another taxi for?' asked Heidler. His mouth opened a little as it always did when he was surprised.

Marya said: 'I'm only going home to get some things. I'm going back to the Rue Tollman; I'm going to stay with my husband while he's in Paris, naturally.'

'Naturally!' she repeated, staring hardly at Lois.

She rapped on the glass in front. The driver looked round. She rapped again and he stopped. She opened the door for herself and got down.

'Good night,' she said and shut the door on them. She ran up to the nearest taxi. 'First to the Hôtel Bosphore, then to the Rue Tollman, number – I'll stop you.'

As she spoke, she was thinking with agony: Heidler! Heidler!

'Extraordinary thing to do,' remarked Heidler. He was very pale.

Lois said: 'Yes. Monsieur Zelli is a funny little man, isn't he? But she's obviously very fond of him.'

He was silent.

She went on in a low voice: 'My poor H. J. Oh, my poor, poor H. J. All this is so abominably sordid.'

She looked sharply at him as she spoke, then out of the window at the wet streets.

'That's that,' she thought. And suddenly she felt weak, exhausted like someone at the end of a long and terrible effort. Tears came into her eyes. She blinked, pressed her lips together, and told herself again: 'Yes, that's that.'

*

It was very quiet in the room at the hotel in the Rue Tollman. Only the gentle sound of falling rain came up from the dark street outside.

'You don't love me any more,' said Stephan. 'I feel it. I know it. You stiffen when I touch you. Well, I don't blame you. A year in jail doesn't make a man appetizing.'

'I'm awfully tired,' said Marya, 'and awfully sad. Will you just be kind to me for a little? And don't let's think about love at all. You know, sometimes I'm so sad! Life is

141

so hard and puzzling, awful, it seems to me. If I could rest just for a bit. I'm longing to rest for a bit.'

He said gently: 'Don't worry. *T'en fais pas!*' He put his arms round her. 'Can't you sleep like that? Are you well like that?'

'Oh, yes,' she sighed. And slept at once, rocked by the sound of the rain.

The next few days passed like a dream. Lovely days, fresh, and washed and clean. And the knowledge that this was the irrevocable end of their life in Paris made every moment vivid, clearly cut and very sweet. Those were strange days, detached from everything that had gone before or would follow after.

On their last evening they dined recklessly in the Restaurant Chinois of the Rue de l'Ecole de Médécine.

As they began the meal Stephan remarked: 'I've just enough money left for my fare to Amsterdam and a hundred francs for when I get there.' Marya was silent. Then he said: 'Your friends the Heidlers don't like me.'

'Oh yes, they do,' Marya answered feebly. She was taken aback. It was the first time he had mentioned the Heidlers since their meeting.

'And to tell you the truth. . . . What wine shall we drink? Here's a good Sauternes. I suppose you still like Sauternes? To tell you the truth I care as little as I care what's happened to my first shirt whether they like me or not.'

'Stephan,' she asked, 'tell me what you think about Lois.' She waited for his answer nervously as if a great deal depended on it.

'Madame Heidler? I think she is absolutely primitive.'

'You think she's primitive?' Marya repeated slowly. 'You don't think that she might be — very clever?'

'Look here, Mado,' said Stephan, shrugging, 'I've only met Madame Heidler once for a short time, I can't tell you all that. Primitive people follow their instinct and sometimes that's the cleverest thing one can do. Why do you ask me? Madame Heidler is a woman who could be cruel, I think, and very hypocritical, but I saw her squeeze your hand under the table, so I can only suppose that she likes you very much.'

'Oh, she often does that,' said Marya.

Silence.

Then she added, with an effort: 'Don't let's talk about them, don't let's spoil our last evening.'

'No, don't let's spoil it,' said Stephan.

After they had dined they went upstairs to the red-lit bar where several Chinese students were dancing with very blonde women long past their first youth. The students strutted past in a stiffly correct way, melancholy for the sake of dignity, but obviously highly pleased with themselves. At intervals the lights were lowered and a good-looking young violinist played sentimental music on muted strings, and occasionally the something-or-other girls, four of them, pranced in and did a few acrobatics in strict time.

'Wait a moment,' said Stephan. 'I'm going to talk to that boy, I know him.'

'What boy?'

'The violinist.'

He crossed the room and began a long conversation.

At the next table a little flat-faced Japanese was drawing

on the tablecloth and she longed to see what he was doing. The problem of her existence had got beyond her, her brain had given up grappling with it. She stared curiously, absorbed, at her neighbour's thin beautiful hands.

The violinist, finishing his smiling conversation with Stephan, placed his violin under his chin with affection and began to play. It seemed to Marya that the music he played had fate in it. And what was there to catch on to in life but that same idea of fate? A dark river that swept you on you didn't know where – nobody knew where. What was the use of worrying, anyway? *Nitchevo*! 'And have another *fine*, for the Lord's sake.' It was Stephan asking her to have another *fine*.

The Japanese at the next table got up and left. She could lean over and and look at his drawings, which were of elongated and gracefully perverse little women.

'It's a funny thing,' said Stephan, 'that Russian song that the violinist is playing, I had it on the brain when I was in Fresnes. Oh, it's called in French *Par Pitié*. I asked him to play it. I absolutely had it on the brain; I made up words to it.' He looked at the clock above the buffet. 'It's eleven o'clock. If I want to get a seat in the third-class carriage we must go. And I must call at the hotel for my bag.'

In the taxi she turned to him to say: 'Stephan, don't leave me here. For God's sake, take me with you.' But before she could speak, he was talking to her: 'Yes, only just the money for the fare and a very little over.' He spoke as if he had half forgotten her, as if his mind had leaped forward and was already in Amsterdam. 'Oh, I expect I'll be able to manage something,' he said.

'I expect you will,' answered Marya mechanically.

The Gare du Nord was dimly lit, gigantic in the half light. . . .

'I'm not going to wait to see your train out,' she said when he had found a seat. 'It's unlucky and I do so want good luck for you, my dear. Good-bye.'

She kissed him and walked away, turning round several times to wave her hand.

She stood for a moment outside the station looking about her with a bewildered, undecided expression. Then she walked up to a taxi stand. 'Hôtel du Bosphore, Place du Maine, please.'

She rang the night bell and was let in. She looked in the letter-rack. There were no letters.

Then she mounted the stairs to her room, where green-yellow and dullish mauve flowers crawled over the black walls.

She undressed, and all the time she was undressing it was as if Heidler were sitting there watching her with his cool eyes that confused and hurt her.

She lay down. For perhaps thirty seconds she was able to keep her mind a blank; then her obsession gripped her, arid, torturing, gigantic, possessing her as utterly as the longing for water possesses someone who is dying of thirst.

19

MARYA ASKED: 'Any letters for me?'

'Nothing, Madame,' answered the patron, smiling. Smiling? No, grinning was the word. Hateful man. He always grinned when he looked at her. She kept her mouth steady with an effort and stood in the hall putting on her gloves deliberately.

Four days of this. Four days can be a long time.

Across the street was a tobacco shop where they sold pneumatiques. She went there, bought a card and wrote to Heidler, standing at the counter.

My dear,
   I want to see you as soon as possible. Please.

When she had posted the pneumatique she felt relieved, but numb and grey, like a soul in limbo. Four days can be interminable. She lunched, sat for a long while over her coffee, walked for an hour.

When she got back to the hotel, he had answered: 'Can you come to the Versailles about nine this evening? I'll be waiting for you.'

'I must pull myself together,' thought Marya. She was trembling all over. Even her legs were trembling.

As she was dressing, a letter from Stephan arrived. Things weren't going well, he wrote. He might have to leave Amsterdam and go farther on. An evasive letter, which she read indifferently, almost impatiently, finding in it an echo of her own indifference. She put it away in a drawer and went on with her careful preparations.

'Sit here,' said Heidler, 'and have a *café fine*.' He gave her a cold sidelong look. 'Did you see your husband off?'

'Yes.'

'He's gone to Amsterdam, hasn't he?'

She nodded.

A waiter with a benevolent eye brought the coffee and brandies. From the farther side of the café, where Jimmie's Jazz performed nightly, the sound of music reached them faintly, as it were with regret.

'Are you vexed with me?' asked Marya.

'Not at all,' answered Heidler. He cleared his throat. 'My dear Mado . . .' He began to talk dispassionately and deliberately. He spoke with dignity and with a certain relief, as though he were saying something which he had often longed to say. Towards the end of his explanation he became definite, even brutal, though not to excess. All the time that he was speaking she was looking into his eyes. Then she said slowly:

'You're horribly treacherous, Heidler. I suppose you can't help it. I don't suppose you even know it. But you are.'

'I'm not being treacherous; I'm being cruel perhaps,' he added, not without complacency. 'But I'm not being treacherous. I've never shared a woman in my life, not knowingly anyhow, and I'm not going to start now.'

He folded his arms over his chest and looked across into one of the mirrors.

'You forced me to share you,' said Marya, 'for months. Openly and ridiculously. You used your wife to torture me with.'

He answered coldly: 'I don't know what you mean.'

And she saw that it was true.

Then she said: 'But, H. J., I – I love you.'

'You haven't behaved as though you did,' answered Heidler. 'And it's too late now.' He began to talk again – more emphatically, as if her persistence irritated him.

'How cold it is in here,' said Marya when he stopped.

The odd thing was that sitting on a café bench opposite was a little man whom she had met when she first came to Paris five years before, a little, yellow, wizened man and his name was – she couldn't remember – something like Monferrat, Monlisson, Mon. . . . something.

It seemed to her enormously important that she should remember the name of the little man who, staring at her, was obviously also thinking: 'Who is she, where have I met her?'

She couldn't see his face clearly. There was a mist round it. Her hands were so cold that she felt them through the thin stuff of her dress. Mon. Monvoisin, that was it.

Heidler was saying in a low voice: 'I have a horror of you. When I think of you I feel sick.'

He was large, invulnerable, perfectly respectable. Funny to think that she had lain in his arms and shut her eyes because she dared no longer look into his so terribly and wonderfully close. She began to laugh. After all, what did you do when the man you loved said a thing like that? You laughed, obviously.

She said, still laughing: 'So this is the *café fine* of rupture.'

'It is,' said Heidler; 'don't get hysterical about it.'

'Why hysterical?' asked Marya. 'I can laugh if I want to, I suppose. You're funny enough to make anybody laugh sometimes.'

'Of course, laugh. Laugh, but don't cry at the same time.'

'Oh, am I crying?' she said, surprised. She put her hand up to her face.

Monsieur Monvoisin was gazing at her with an expression of avid curiosity. She began to remember all about Monsieur Monvoisin. He was one of Stephan's friends. They had been out together one night, the four of them; Monsieur Monvoisin had brought a girl called Lisette and they had wandered from bar to bar till four o'clock in the morning. A very tall young man had joined the party, who had hummed '*Si j'étais roi*' all the time. The jingling tune began to run in her head.

'Awfully funny,' she remarked to Heidler; 'do you see that man opposite? Well, I know him and he knows me. And he knows, I'm sure, that you are *plaquéing* me. And so does the waiter. Isn't *plaquer* a good word?'

'Very,' he said. 'Now pull yourself together, because we've got several things to talk about.' He looked away from her and added uncomfortably: 'You haven't got to worry, you know.'

'What?' said Marya. 'Oh, yes. Well, you can write to me about that. Let's go now, shall we?'

He seemed surprised and taken aback and made a feeble detaining gesture.

'Wait a minute, wait a minute.'

She turned and looked at him, and when he saw her eyes

he put his hand up to his tie, fidgeted with it and said: 'Oh God! Oh God!'

She passed her tongue over her dry lips, put her handkerchief into her bag and shut it carefully.

He began talking again, hurriedly and uncertainly.

'Look here, Marya, don't suppose . . . I want you to go down South to get well, to forget everything and get well. It's the only thing, believe me. Will you?'

'No,' said Marya.

'Well, I beg you to.'

'No.'

'Why not?'

'I'm very tired,' Marya said, 'I want to go.'

Outside the café he told her: 'Get your things packed,' then he turned and left her.

*

Marya walked straight ahead, her face stiff and set, across the boulevard which looked to her as if it were blazing with lights, on fire with lights, across the Place du Maine and up the avenue.

When she passed under the railway bridge where the cobblestones are always black and glistening, and the walls ooze with damp, she felt for the first time a definite sensation of loss and pain, and tears came into her eyes. She walked on with the fixed idea that if she went far enough she would reach some obscure, dark cavern away from the lights and the passers-by. Surely at the end of this long and glaring row of lamps she would find it, the friendly dark where she could lie and let her heart burst. And as she walked she was certain that every woman she passed was mocking her gleefully and every man she passed was mocking her contemptuously. After a time she felt tired and went into a café, a vast echoing place, nearly empty. The electric lights were arranged in a square pattern overhead and for some reason this made the place look like a casino. The orchestra was seated on a raised platform in the middle of the room; it had just finished playing *The Huguenots*, and the pianist, in spectacles, leaned forward arranging the music of *The Barber of Seville* with a fussy, conscientious look on her face. Jazz was far from her well-ordered mind.

As Marya was drinking the brandy she had ordered, the music blared forth. It echoed lugubriously in that barn of a place, and a young man who was writing letters at the next table looked up with a pained expression, sighed and pushed away his blotter; then he proceeded to stare with interest at Marya.

She paid the waiter, got up and went out, and he followed her, leaving money on the table. When he spoke to her she looked up at him with vacant eyes. He repeated his question:

'Why are you sad?'

'I'm not sad,' answered Marya mechanically; 'I'm tired.' But now she walked to the rhythm of the words.

'Why are you sad? *Pourquoi êtes-vous triste? Pourquoi? Pourquoi?*'

The young man by her side began to talk. He told her all sorts of things. That he had been born in Tonkin, that his nurse had had a name which meant spouse. That most of the Annamite women seemed to have a name which meant spouse. That his family had returned to France when he was nine years of age. To Toulon. That was ten years ago. That he, also, was sad as his mistress had betrayed him.

'I ought to know better by this time. Nevertheless, I'm sad. I know what it is to love.' As he talked he observed her carefully, glancing sideways. 'If you're tired,' he said at last, 'won't you come to my room and rest?' He took her firmly by the arm. 'I live not so far away – in the Rue Racine. You must come up to my room and rest.'

'Why not?' said Marya. 'What's it matter?'

She laughed suddenly, and when she laughed the young man looked surprised, even shocked. Then he gripped her arm more firmly and led her across the road to a taxi. She went with him silently – like a sleep-walker.

When they got to his room she said: 'Oh, but I don't like the light. Light hurts me.'

'Well,' answered the young man, 'don't worry about that. I'll soon arrange that.'

He went to a drawer and produced two enormous blue silk handkerchiefs, which he proceeded to tie round the electric light.

'I've often noticed,' he continued, 'that women, for one reason or another. . . . *Enfin.*'

20

HEIDLER SAID: 'Well, are your things packed?' He walked across to the window and flung it wider open. 'Much too hot in here.'

'I'm not going,' said Marya stubbornly. She was lying huddled on the bed and he sat on a chair near her and took her hand in his.

'How cold you are.'

His eyes were very cautious. He was thinking that it wouldn't do to leave the girl trailing round Montparnasse looking as ill as all that. She was lying huddled. As if there were a spring broken somewhere. He felt at once flattered, impatient and pitiful.

He said, speaking very gently, that he had arranged everything. The train next day at twelve, the night at Lyons. 'And you'll be in Cannes the following morning.'

'I'm not going,' repeated Marya.

'You'll like Cannes,' said Heidler persuasively. 'Sure to. Everybody likes Cannes. Well, I mean everybody wants to be there. And you can stay some days at Cannes and look round for somewhere else.'

'I won't go,' Marya said in a high voice. 'I won't go. Leave me alone.'

She jumped up. Her felt hat was lying on the floor and she gave it a violent kick.

'Leave me alone!'

Heidler looked at her sharply, then picked the hat up, smoothed it and put it on the table. He said:

'Don't worry about your things. I'll tell the maid here to pack for you. She'll do it all right. Come out and have something to eat. We'll ring for her before we go.'

He walked up to her and put his hands on her shoulders. When he touched her, she flushed scarlet and her mouth twitched.

'There, there, there!' said Heidler soothingly. 'It's all right. It's all right. Come along. Put your hat on. . . .'

21

THE BEACH WAS strewn with old sardine tins and fishing nets spread to dry in the sun. A little white boat, called *Je m'en fous*, heaved very slowly up and down at the end of its rope. Beyond the pebbles and the sardine tins the sea was the colour of a field of blue hyacinths.

Marya lay in the sun hour after hour and her thoughts were vague and pale, like ghosts. At the back of the beach a sparse line of eucalyptus trees danced gaily in the wind. Sometimes a brown, sturdy fisherwoman or a thin yellow dog would pass and look down on her, lying motionless with one arm over her eyes.

'But you ought to go to Nice, Madame,' said the landlady of the Hôtel des Palmiers. She was pretty, dark and fat, and she enjoyed relating the complicated history of her inside. '*Hélas*! What it is to be a woman,' she would say at the finish.

'I don't like Nice,' answered Marya.

'The tram stops outside the door every twenty minutes,' continued the landlady, ignoring, as was proper, her client's last foolish remark.

'Well,' said Marya suddenly, 'I'll go this afternoon; why not?'

In Nice the sun blazed down on the white houses along the sea front and the strong-winged gulls swooped and dived gracefully, and the stone ladies smiled complacently from the front of the Hôtel Negresco, as if to say: 'Think what you like, curves are charming.' There was a sort of sweet reasonableness in the very air; everything logical, arranged, purposeful, under a surface of grace, lightness and gaiety. Life as it should be lived.

Marya sat in an empty café out of the sun and looked for a long time at the blank sheet of writing paper in front of her, imagining it covered with words, black marks on the white paper. Words. To make somebody understand.

'I must make him understand,' she thought. Then wrote slowly:

Dear Heidler,

I am horribly unhappy. I'm simply going mad down here. When I think of you and Lois together I really feel as if I were going mad. You don't believe me. I can see you smiling. But it's true. It's as if all the blood in my body is being drained, very slowly, all the time, all the blood in my heart. What can I say to make you believe me? I can't think properly any more. I'm fichue. Please be patient with me. But I want to go back to Paris; I shouldn't have come down here. Surely you must see that. I mean, will you send enough money for me to go back to Paris and live there for a week or two? That's all I want of you. It was like drinking something very bitter to the last drop when I wrote that. And now I know that I'm nothing at all. Nothing. Nothing. But I did love you. If I were dying, that would be the last thing I would say, that I loved you. That's one of the things that torments me that I don't believe you ever knew how much I loved you. Well, and I can see you smiling at all this. My dear, my dear, for God's sake, send me the money at once and let me go. I'm being tormented here. Please.

'That's a rotten letter,' thought Marya. She sighed and asked the waiter for more paper. And, seeing that he looked sulky: 'And another *café crême*, take this one away.'

The waiter looked at the first glass of coffee, cold and untouched, raised his eyebrows, shrugged his shoulders and departed, dragging his feet. As she waited for him, Marya watched a fierce-eyed, beak-nosed girl opposite who was also writing rapidly. As she wrote, tears came to her eyes. Probably a letter of rupture. When the waiter came back with the coffee and the paper Marya had addressed her letter.

'I can't write it again,' she thought.

She paid him and went out, leaving him staring after her and smiling. But as soon as she had posted her incoherent epistle she felt relieved and even peaceful. She went back to the Hôtel des Palmiers and lay in her bedroom with her eyes shut, thinking: 'I ought to have an answer in four or five days. I must have an answer.'

It was a large bedroom with a stone-flagged floor, and the palm trees leant in a friendly fashion almost through the windows of the room. Outside in the passage the little *bonne*, Marya's namesake, sang as she mopped the floor. She was sixteen years of age, and pretty with a soft, warm, broad-browed prettiness. She sang, she mopped, she minded the *patronne*'s baby, who on its unformed legs wobbled about in an extraordinary wooden contraption on wheels.

*

A few mornings later the *patronne* knocked at Marya's door to say:

'A lady to see you, Madame. She's in the garden.'

'Good morning,' said Miss Nicolson with an efficient smile. 'Lois asked me to look you up.'

Marya greeted her, then threw a desperate glance backwards into the hotel with a wild idea of escaping this reincarnation of her torment.

Miss Nicolson stood sturdily in the sun, long-bodied, short-legged, neat, full of common sense, grit, pep and all the rest. She was dressed in grey; she wore a green scarf and a becoming hat. Her small feet were shod with crocodile-skin shoes. It was oddly shocking to catch glimpses of very hairy legs through her thin silk stockings.

'I'm staying at Antibes,' said Miss Nicolson. 'I had Lois's letter about you this morning.'

Her eyes travelled rapidly upwards and downwards gathering information, searching hopefully for the inevitable weak point. Marya muttered an invitation to luncheon and the other looked doubtfully into the dark dining-room of the hotel.

'We can go to the zoo,' suggested Marya, 'it's quite close by. Some Russian people have a restaurant there.'

As they walked down the sunny road, Miss Nicolson chattered gaily about Lois Heidler, about Heidler, ('Dreadful man!' said Miss Nicolson), about Lois's extraordinary affection for Marya.

They lunched in the sun on heavy Russian food. It was very hot. There was a pungent smell of animals in the air.

Miss Nicolson still discoursed, gradually approaching her climax: Montparnasse, her darling Lois, the husband of her darling Lois, men in general, men who get sick of their mistresses and send them away into the country to get rid of them.

Marya listened with a curiously helpless feeling. It was as if bandages were being torn from an unhealed wound.

'Lois thought, when she read your last letter to them, that you must be seedy.'

'To them?'

'Yes,' said Miss Nicolson innocently, but with a shrewd sidelong look. 'You did write to them saying you were ill or something, didn't you?' She added after a pause: 'Lois told me to tell you that H. J.'s very busy just now, but that she'll see that he answers your letter in a day or two.'

Marya paid for the meal in silence with the last hundred francs in her purse.

Miss Nicolson, looking away into the blue distance, remarked: 'Women are pitiful, I do think.' Then, because she was light of touch and by no means hard-hearted, she stopped talking about Montparnasse. She said that she despised women from the Southern states because they weren't efficient. She said that her mother had divorced her father and that 'all we children sympathized with mother, all of us.' Father, it seemed, was from South Carolina and shiftless. She said that that marvellous blue made her feel peaceful, that she adored Beauty, that she lived for Beauty.

Marya looked at her curiously. It was strange to think that Miss Nicolson adored beauty and yearned and all the rest. Because she looked such a tightly packed, shrewd-eyed little person. But obviously she did yearn, for here she was saying so.

'I don't leap to it any more, though,' said Miss Nicolson sadly. 'I used to leap to beauty, but not now.'

159

'Let's go and look at the animals,' suggested Marya.

There was a young fox in a cage at the end of the zoo – a cage perhaps three yards long. Up and down it ran, up and down, and Marya imagined that each time it turned it did so with a certain hopefulness, as if it thought that escape was possible. Then, of course, there were the bars. It would strike its nose, turn and run again. Up and down, up and down, ceaselessly. A horrible sight, really.

'Sweet thing,' said Miss Nicolson.

'You know, one sometimes takes great dislikes to people who aren't at all what one imagines they are,' said Miss Nicolson. 'People often aren't, are they?'

'Yes,' agreed Marya. 'I mean, no, they aren't. Will you come back to the hotel for some coffee? They'll know the trains to Antibes. Or there's a 'bus from Cagnes every half-hour.'

She was thinking: 'I must get drunk tonight. I must get so drunk that I can't walk, so drunk that I can't see.'

Miss Nicolson decided on a train about six.

'Good-bye,' she said, as she leapt lightly up the high carriage-step with her scarf fluttering bravely behind her. 'Will you come and lunch with me at Antibes next week – say Tuesday?'

'Yes,' said Marya. 'Of course. Good-bye.'

After the fifth Pernod drunk at the little café on the beach Marya thought: 'It's as if I were drinking water. Never mind.'

At the hotel she made a pretence of dining, then went

up to her room and took several cachets of veronal. As soon as she lay down she slept. It was still light.

At about two o'clock in the morning she awoke moaning. She lay very still for a moment, then sat up in bed with tightly pressed lips. Every muscle in her body was taut.

'Hold on! Don't be a fool,' she said to herself.

She lay back and shut her eyes and saw Heidler kneeling down to pray in the little church and looking sideways at her to see if she were impressed. He got up and walked out of the church into the room. 'God's a pal of mine,' he said. 'He probably looks rather like me, with cold eyes and fattish hands. I'm in His image or He's in mine. It's all one. I prayed to Him to get you and I got you. Shall I give you a letter of introduction? Yes, I might do that if you remind me. No trouble at all. Now then, don't be hysterical. Besides, Lois was there first. Lois is a good woman and you are a bad one; it's quite simple. These things are. That's what is meant by having principles. Nobody owes a fair deal to a prostitute. It isn't done. My dear girl, what would become of things if it were? Come, come to think it over. Intact or not intact, that's the first question. An income or not an income, that's the second.'

Then she found herself thinking with lucidity: 'He gave her my letter to read, of course. It's like being stripped and laughed at.'

She put the light on and looked at the red marks on her arm, where her teeth had nearly met. 'And I haven't got a dress with long sleeves, either.'

She worried about that for a while, then got up and arranged the bedclothes carefully. Her nightgown was soaked with sweat. She took a fresh one from the cupboard and lay down again with relief. The room had swayed with her when she stood up.

The croaking of frogs came in through the open window and, very faintly, the sound of the sea. Then it was not the sound of the sea, but of trees in a gale. Dark trees growing close together with thick creepers which hung down from the branches like snakes. Virgin forest. Intact. Never been touched.

She sighed because the pillow was so hot, moved uneasily and opened her eyes. She thought: 'What a row the sea is making tonight.' But there was a noise in her head, too, a roaring noise, and the bed kept sinking under her in a sickening fashion. 'I've doped myself properly,' she thought. 'Perhaps if I leaned out of the window.' But she was too giddy to get up. She was too giddy to keep her eyes open. She shut them and again the bed plunged downwards with her – sickeningly – into blackness.

She was trying to climb out of the blackness up an interminable ladder. She was very small, as small as a fly, yet so heavy, so weighted down that it was impossible to hoist herself to the next rung. The weight on her was terrible, the vastness of space round her was terrible. She was going to fall. She was falling. The breath left her body.

'Yes I heard you being sick this morning, Madame,' said Madame Moreau with an inquisitive look.

'I'll just stay in bed today,' explained Marya, 'and then I'll be all right tomorrow. I was—' She stopped, because she realized in time that if she said, 'I was drunk,' Madame

Moreau would be disgusted and shocked to the core. 'I had an awful headache yesterday,' she said. 'I still have.'

'You look ill,' said the *patronne*.

A couple of hours afterwards she came back, had another look at Marya and then remarked: 'If I telephone to Nice for a doctor?' She went away to do it.

The doctor was small and brown and he asked a great many questions in a staccato voice. Then he tapped and pinched and probed with hands that hurt rather.

'I want,' said Marya, 'something to make me sleep. Something rather strong, please. I've been taking veronal, but it makes me sick.'

'Ah?' said the doctor. He wrote out two prescriptions, told her to wear a hat in the sun and went away looking wise.

In two days Heidler replied:

> *Dear Mado,*
>
> *I've had your letter. I cannot for many reasons send you a large sum of money. I certainly do not intend to help you to join your husband and I do not consider that you are well enough to get back to Paris yet. I'm glad Miss Nicolson came to see you. Lois thought she might cheer you up. Here is a cheque for three hundred francs for your hotel this week. Do try to get well.*
>
> *Yours, H.*

She read this letter indifferently. Nothing mattered just then. It was extraordinary that anything had ever mattered at all. Extraordinary and unbelievable that anything had ever mattered.

The days were hot and very lovely. Loveliest in the morning, because then there were grey and silver in the blue dream and cool shadows on the water that was so hot and sticky at midday. Rather like bathing in warmish oil. But sticky or not, it was a caressing sea. If you had any guts; if you were anything else but a tired-out coward, you'd swim out into the blue and never come back. A good way to finish if you'd made a mess of your life.

When she had bathed she would lie and think of little things, stupid things like a yellow dress that Stephan had bought her once at Ostend. He always chose beautiful clothes. He had a flair for that sort of thing. It had been fun to wear beautiful clothes and to feel fresh and young and like a flower. The greatest fun in the world.

One day, quite suddenly, the weather changed and that morning she had a letter from Stephan to say that he was coming back to Paris.

I can't get any work here, he wrote, *I won't tell you how I've been existing for I don't want to depress you, but I've made up my mind that to get right away is my only chance, and I'm going to try for the Argentine. But I want to see you again before I go and that's why I'm coming to Paris. Don't be afraid; there is no risk. I know a man with whom I can stay quite safely and as long as nobody actually denounces me to the police, I am all right. I've managed to borrow eight hundred francs. I am sending four hundred to help you to pay your journey. Come as quickly as you can. I'll let you know an address to wire to.*

Stephan.

She meditated over this letter, seated in the dark dining-room of the Hôtel des Palmiers. The grey sky and the cold were a relief and the mistral galvanized her into some sort of activity. She sat with her chin on her hand, a glass of black coffee before her, and felt a faint stirring of hope.

22

'I'VE GOT A room for you in a hotel near the Gare du Nord,' said Stephan. He took her arm protectingly. 'You're awfully tired, aren't you? Stay here for a moment; give me the *fiche* of your baggage.' It was a grey morning. The sky was the colour of train smoke. 'My friend Jacques Bernadet lives in that quarter,' he explained in the taxi, 'in the Rue Bleue. But I'll tell you afterwards; you must have breakfast and a rest first.'

'Is that where you can hide?' inquired Marya.

'Hide, well, hide,' said Stephan, shrugging. 'As long as I haven't to register, the police won't bother about me.'

'D'you think so?' asked Marya doubtfully.

He was leaning back smoking a cigarette and smiling, his felt hat at the back of his head. When she looked at him she felt reassured. Stephan was like that. He was always able to make his doings appear reasonable. A comforting quality that.

'Well, here we are,' he said. 'You remember that little café just round the corner, don't you? We often used to go there.'

The hotel, which was called the Hôtel de Havane, was brand new. It smelt of paint and there were ladders and pails of whitewash on the staircase. Marya had often wandered about that part of Paris with Stephan when they lived in Montmartre, and she remembered the dingy streets, the vegetable shops kept by sleek-haired women,

166

the bars haunted by gaily dressed little prostitutes who seemed to be perpetually making the gesture of opening their bags to powder their noses. Over the whole of the quarter the sinister and rakish atmosphere of the Faubourg Montmartre spread like some perfume.

Stephan came in to announce that the bath would be ready in half an hour, and that the bathroom was at the end of the corridor. He added that he had not much money left.

'How much have you got?'

'I don't know,' said Marya; 'look in my bag.'

'You have fifty-five francs,' he told her. 'Well, we'll talk about that afterwards.'

He came towards her with open arms and a mouth that looked greedy.

'What did you say?'

'Nothing.'

(She had said: 'Heidler! Heidler!')

'Nothing,' she muttered. 'I'm awfully tired. It was a ghastly journey. The carriage was packed. I couldn't lie down at all.'

'You'll be able to sleep after we've eaten,' he said.

Then he told her that he had promised to meet his benefactor, Monsier Bernadet, and Monsieur Bernadet's girl, that evening at half-past six.

Monsieur Jacques Bernadet was a plump young man of middle height. His face was round, smooth and carefully powdered. He had large-pupilled, long-lashed, blue eyes which he used in a practised and effective manner, a very small pursed mouth and a high tenor voice.

'Madame,' he said, 'I am enchanted to meet you.'

'What a dreadful man!' thought Marya.

But the girl with him (her name, it seemed, was Mademoiselle Simone Chardin) was certainly attractive. Astoundingly pretty indeed. She was young, swarthy, and wore a red dress tightly fitting and long sleeved, buttoning closely up to the throat. She spoke very little.

'I'm here,' her eyes seemed to say, 'because for the moment I can't find anything better to do. But don't try to mix me up too much in your affairs.'

The party sat in a very small café in the Rue Lamartine. There was a bar upstairs and a coal shop in the cellar, an unexpected but usual combination. Through the open door they could see the Place Cadet and its kiosk of flowers, the red back of a newspaper stall, and the open mouth of the Metro station.

Stephan ordered four Pernods.

'We always come here for aperitifs,' he explained to Marya, 'because the man who owns the place is a good type.'

'*Très délicat, cet homme là*,' affirmed Monsieur Bernadet.

He began a long, involved story illustrating the extraordinary delicacy of the *patron*, a heavily moustached individual who sat behind his bar with an immovable face, pouring out the drinks at intervals with a steady hand. The mirror at his back reflected his head, round as a bullet, covered with a coarse mane of hair, and the multi-coloured row of bottles. A hatless woman came in, drank a glass of white wine at the bar counter and inquired after a certain *beau blond*.

'Tell him from me that I'm still waiting for him,' she said and drifted out, laughing.

'I know a type,' said Bernadet, gloomily finishing his Pernod, 'who makes a fortune every three years in the Argentine, and then he comes to Paris to spend it, the fool. Let me once be out of this misery and I wouldn't be back in a hurry, I tell you! My God, Paris. Paris. Well, and then? Without money Paris is as rotten as anywhere else and worse.'

'It's nice all the same, Paris,' murmured the girl.

She had taken off her hat. Her hair, which was curly and worn cut to the neck, fell very beautifully about her face and smelt of some warm perfume. Her mouth was like a child's.

'Paris is the most beautiful place in the world,' she said seriously. 'Everybody knows that.'

Monsieur Bernadet chanted with sarcasm:

> Oh!
> Que c'est beau,
> Mon village-e,
> Mon Paris . . .

'Air connu.'

'What scent do you use?' asked Marya suddenly, speaking to Mademoiselle Chardin. 'Chypre?'

'I? L'Heure Bleue of Guerlain.'

'Guerlain! Listen to that,' said Bernadet. 'I ask you.' He gave a short laugh like a bark. 'Guerlain!'

'You get on my nerves,' answered the girl with calm dignity.

Stephan suggested more Pernod and, as Mademoiselle Chardin refused, three more apéritifs were ordered and the two men discussed the Argentine with gravity.

You could make your way there, it seemed, provided that you turned your back on the towns. The country was the thing. Ranches. Cattle.

'But you can't ride,' said Mademoiselle Chardin to her friend. 'You're talking about ranches and you've never been on the back of a horse in your life.'

'One learns that quickly,' answered Monsieur Bernadet hopefully. 'Besides, there are other jobs to be had on ranches, aren't there? They want cashiers, for instance.'

He spoke without smiling. Marya had a swift vision of Monsieur Bernadet clad in the becoming costume of a cowboy, escaping with the cash box of some confiding ranch owner under his arm. Rolling down to Rio as it were. But it would have to be a very confiding ranch owner indeed, she thought.

After the third round of apéritifs, Monsieur Bernadet rose and, bowing politely, remarked that Stephan doubtless wished to conduct his lady to dine somewhere.

'The *prix fixe* place round the corner is not bad,' he advised. 'Three francs fifty, wine included. *A tout à l'heure, mon vieux.*'

'I don't like that man,' said Marya at once. 'Where ever did you get hold of him?'

Stephan twirled his empty glass in his fingers with a moody expression.

'I knew him at the Santé. He was my left-hand neighbour, and when we went out to take exercise in the courtyard I spoke one or two words to him. Then we telephoned to each other. You don't know that there is a telephone system in the prison, naturally. Well, I'd forgotten all about him, when we met by chance in Rotterdam, and he told me that if I wanted to come to Paris I could stay at his place quietly without anyone knowing it. I understand quite well,' he added with bitterness, 'that these are not the sort of people you like, but *voilà*. I don't think any respectable gentleman would risk lending me his flat, and I have to take what I can get in the way of friends.'

'You're quite wrong,' answered Marya, 'about the sort of people I like, only I wouldn't trust this particular man very far, if I were you.'

Stephan remarked scornfully: 'Trust! You're funny with your trust. No, of course, I don't trust him, any more than I trust anybody else. I make use of him and that's all. Let's go and eat.'

After dinner, in the evil-smelling little restaurant, Stephan said suddenly:

'You understand, don't you, that I must get away? I've lost my luck. I care too much. I did my best but it was no good. I've lost my luck.'

His mouth drooped at the corners. There was something wolf-life about his sharpened features. He went on:

'I can't any more. You don't know what it is. I can't. I've cried myself to sleep like a little boy night after night. Well, and what's the use of that? One stays and cries, that's all. And there's so much that I want to forget and so much that I don't dare to think of. I'm not myself any more. Life is pressing on me all the time. Constantly. To doubt everything. My God, it's horrible, I must get away. If I could get away, I might be myself again. There's an emigration bureau at Genoa. I'm going there. . . . *Partir. Partir.* To get away,' he muttered.

She said: 'Stephan, look here. Don't leave me. All the

way to Paris I was thinking that I'd tell you this. Don't leave me, please. Take me with you. We needn't go to the Argentine, need we? Because that would be horribly expensive. But there are lots of other places. It isn't impossible if you really want it. Nothing is.'

He told her: 'You don't know what it is, *la misère*. Nobody knows what it is till it's got them.'

Marya looked away and answered slowly: 'No. That's true. Nobody knows what it is till it's got them. But suppose that I could borrow some money. I might be able to.'

He gave her a sidelong look. 'Bernadet says that he may be able to lend me some in a week.'

'Oh, Bernadet,' said Marya impatiently. 'I don't believe a word of that.'

'Neither do I,' confessed Stephan.

Silence.

'I must be somewhere where I can work,' he muttered. 'People talk, but let them be in my situation and they would see. My God! to go smash, to go right under for want of a little money.'

She looked at him, and said in a very low voice: 'I'll write to . . . I'll write . . . or perhaps there's a letter for me at the Hôtel du Bosphore.'

After that they talked again about Monsieur Bernadet. His business, it seemed, was the enlargement of photographs. Marya said that she didn't know that anybody ever wanted their photographs enlarged these days.

'Well, they don't,' said Stephan. 'Hardly anybody. But that's supposed to be his business. Well, shall we go along to see them now?'

*

The three rooms where Bernadet and Mademoiselle Chardin lived were on the third floor of a dark and dilapidated house in the Rue Bleue. Stephan remarked as they went upstairs: 'The concierge hates Bernadet, I shall have to be careful of her. She sympathizes with his wife. You know, Bernadet chased his wife, sent her off.'

'What? When he met this girl?' asked Marya innocently.

'This girl? Oh no, another one; this one is nothing. Bernadet met her at the Moulin Rouge the other night and she had nowhere to go, nowhere to sleep. So he asked her to come back with him.'

'She's awfully pretty,' said Marya.

Stephan answered indifferently: 'Oh, she's a good girl. My coat was torn and she mended it very nicely. She's fed up with Bernadet. But I mean, I must be careful of the concierge.'

Mademoiselle Chardin opened the door and led the way into a high-ceilinged room where a great many gigantic photographs — mostly family groups — stared down from the walls. There was a dusty counter down the middle of it and piles of cardboard boxes in the corner. It was crowded with odds and ends of furniture. A place like a bric-à-brac shop, smelling of dust and of Mademoiselle Chardin's perfume.

23

'YOU THINK TOO much,' said Monsieur Bernadet kindly. 'That's what's the matter with you. When I saw you last night I said to myself: "That's a pretty girl, but a girl who thinks too much." For instance, just now when I passed, what were you thinking of?'

Marya said: 'The newspaper kiosk.'

'Ah?' He lifted supple eyebrows.

She explained: 'I like sitting on the terrace of a café near a kiosk and looking at the names of the newspapers. Can you see? *Magyar Hirlap*, *Svenska*, *Poochi*, *Pesti Hirlap*. I like looking at them ranged one under the other because—' She stopped and shrugged a little.

'Evidently,' remarked Monsieur Bernadet, 'it's an amusement like another.'

('My God, what a neurasthenic!' he was thinking. 'But she has beautiful eyes.')

'To tell you the truth,' he continued, 'I have no curiosity at all about other countries. None. After all, what can I find in other countries that I can't find better in France? Of course, if one went to make money it would be different.'

'Evidently,' answered Marya in her turn. 'A Pernod fils, please. One pretends that one will find something different. It's only a game.'

Bernadet said, after a silence: 'Stephan is waiting for

174

you at the Rue Bleue. You know that he'll be alone there for a few days. Do you drink that without water?'

'Yes,' answered Marya. And, 'Yes, Stephan told me that you were going away this evening. You've been kind to him, Monsieur Bernadet. Thank you.'

'It's nothing at all,' muttered the other. 'One does what one can for a comrade.'

He fidgeted, then drew his chair closer and went on in a mysterious voice.

'And if I tell you that Stephan ought to leave Paris as quickly as possible, I say it for his sake. Yes. And the less he goes out while he is here the better. A man thinks, "I'm quite safe. Nobody is bothering about me." He goes out; someone who knows him sees him on the boulevard and – there you are. Next day the police. People are *vache*, people play dirty tricks for no reason at all. That's life.'

'Perhaps it makes them feel warm and comfortable,' suggested Marya.

Monsieur Bernadet said: 'What? Well, it's no use making philosophy about these things. Nearly everybody will be *vache* if you give them a chance; the best way is not to give them a chance. That's life.'

'You understand,' he went on after a pause, 'that it's not my business. I'm going away and if anything happens, it will not be seen, not known as far as I'm concerned.'

'I bet it will,' thought Marya. But she liked him better than she had done.

He finished his apéritif.

'Well, Madame, I hope to see you when I come back. Don't worry too much. Stephan is a clever boy and energetic. Anybody who looks at him can see that. He

175

won't stay long in *la misère*. But, of course, if he can have a little money to help him so much the better. People may talk,' said Monsieur Bernadet, 'but without money – without any money at all – well.'

He pressed his lips together and shook his head several times. Then he rapped for the waiter, paid and got up.

She watched him walking up the street. He wore a very tight brown overcoat cut in at the waist. He sidled past people who got in his way with peculiar eel-like motions of his shoulders.

'Perhaps when I've sat here for a while,' Marya told herself, 'I'll be able to think better. Can't think now. So damn tired.'

Her brain was working slowly and confusedly; it seemed at moments to stop working altogether.

'But I've lots of time,' she assured herself again. 'Lots. Hours and hours.'

She stared at the newspaper kiosk and again began to imagine herself in the train, thudding across the great plain of Europe. With Stephan. Hundreds of miles of plain for the wind to sweep over.

Stephan. He looked so thin and his eyes were horribly sad. She remembered him saying, 'I cried like a little boy,' and her heart twisted with pity.

The tears came into her eyes and she told herself: 'That's this damned apéritif. I must pull myself together; I must think properly.' She pushed the glass, which was still half full, away from her.

After a time she took Heidler's letter out of her bag and looked at it. He had written: 'I'm sending this to the

Hôtel du Bosphore and hope you'll get it. I'm worried about you. Why have you come back to Paris so suddenly? Will you let me know where and when we can meet? I am only too anxious to do all I can to help you. Please believe that.'

When and where? In some café, of course. The unvarying background. Knowing waiters, clouds of smoke, the smell of drink. She would sit there trembling, and he would be cool, a little impatient, perhaps a little nervous. Then she would try to explain and he would listen with a calm expression. Top dog.

'Of course you want money,' he would be thinking. 'Naturally. How much? I'm willing to give the traditional sum, the sum which is right and proper under the circumstances, and no more. Well, talk. I'm listening.'

She'd talk and all the time her eyes would be saying, 'I loved you. I loved you. D'you remember?'

But he wouldn't look at her eyes, or if he did he'd look away again very quickly. He'd be feeling healthy-minded, outrageously so. He'd long for cold baths and fresh air. Can't she explain and get it over?

'Didn't I tell her that she made me feel sick? The extraordinary persistence of this type of woman.'

Explain? But she couldn't explain. She'd have to be clever and cunning, or she wouldn't get any money at all.

'I've got to be clever,' she thought, 'clever.' Then again something in her head clicked and jarred like a rundown machine. It was cold on the café terrace. She began to shiver.

'Must be pretty late. I've been here a long time.'

She opened her bag, put away Heidler's letter, paid the waiter and walked away, moving stiffly.

'I can't any more – I can't. I must be comforted. I can't any more. I can't any more. Can't go on. Can't . . .'

*

Stephan had spread the table with cold sausage cut into slices, potato salad, a bottle of wine and a half-emptied bottle of rum. The huge photographs stared down at them with glassy eyes.

They ate in silence. She noticed that the cardboard boxes had disappeared and that he must have spent a long time trying to make the room look tidy. He had a mania for order, had Stephan.

When the meal was over Marya cleared away the plates and piled them in the kitchen.

She said to him when she came back: 'Stephan, listen. I've something to tell you.'

'Well?'

'I've something to tell you,' she repeated and, turning her eyes away from him, fixed them on a big spider motionless on the dirty white wall.

'What is it, Mado?'

'It's that. . . . D'you love me?' she asked.

'Yes.'

'Really, really?'

'Yes.'

'I'm terribly unhappy,' said Marya.

She knelt down by his chair and put her head on his knees. Then she thought it would be ridiculous to talk to him like that.

'Nothing to kneel about. How perfectly ridiculous!'

She got up, sat in one of the hard, straight-backed chairs, gripped the sides of it and fixed her eyes on the spider.

She said: 'I'm unhappy. Help me, Stephan, do help me.'

'I see that you're unhappy,' he told her gently. 'I want to help you.'

'I found a letter from Heidler at the hotel,' she said. 'I . . . I want to tell you about him . . . and Lois.'

She flushed as she pronounced the name of her enemy. Then she went on in the voice of someone talking aloud in an empty room.

'Yes. There was a letter from him at the hotel today. But first . . . I must tell you. When I'd been there with them . . . a little time, Heidler started making love to me. And so I went to her, to Lois, and I told her what was happening and I asked her to let me have the money to go away. And she said . . . that what was the matter with me was that I was too virtuous and that she didn't mind. And that I was a fool not to trust Heidler. And that night she went out somewhere and left me alone with him.'

She was silent for a while. Then she repeated:

'Lois said: ''What's the matter with you is that you are too virtuous.'' And she went out and left me alone with him. . . .'

He leaned forward, and looking at her with an expression of curiosity, said:

'Mado – did you let Heidler make love to you?'

She answered impatiently: 'Wait and let me tell you. When she said that, I knew she was lying, but I despised her, hated her for lying, and I made up my mind not to

179

think about her any more. And I was awfully tired. You don't know. . . . I was tired. He kept saying, "I love you." Over and over again. Just "I love you, I love you, my dear." And I loved him too,' she whispered. 'I loved him too – quite suddenly.'

Then she was silent for a moment.

'Listening outside the door.' she went on. 'Putting on carpet slippers and creeping up outside the door to listen.'

'Who did, Heidler?'

'No, she did. She used to put on carpet slippers and come and listen at the door. She said "What's the matter with you is that you're too virtuous." I swear to God she said that. And she sneered. She was always sneering. She has that sort of mouth. You don't know how often I've lain awake and longed . . . to smash her mouth so that she could never sneer again.'

He listened to this incoherent speech without moving, but when she was silent.

'When did all this happen?' he asked.

Marya thought how ugly his voice sounded. 'What am I doing here with this man?' she thought. 'This foreigner with his ugly voice?'

'It happened,' she said vaguely, 'oh, quite soon. And they wanted me to go on staying with them, but I wouldn't because I heard them whispering together one night about me. That was why I went to the hotel.'

'You mean to say,' said Stephan, 'that all the time you used to come and see me in jail you were Heidler's mistress? You used to come and laugh at me, well put away behind the bars so that I couldn't interfere?'

'I didn't come to laugh at you. Oh, no! But I wish

you'd listen,' she exclaimed fretfully. 'You keep stopping me. And I want to tell you.'

'I'm listening,' said Stephan. 'I'm listening. You can go on.'

'She said to me: "What's the matter with you is that you're too virtuous." ' Then again she was silent. An expression of hatred convulsed her face.

'But what's the use,' interrupted Stephan, 'of going on about what Heidler's wife told you? She did the best for herself and I don't blame her. D'you think she's the only woman who shuts her eyes? More than shuts her eyes if necessary. Come! Don't be a fool. If you were so naïve you have only yourself to blame. When you went to the hotel, Heidler came to see you? When did he come? Often?'

'No, I don't remember,' said Marya vaguely. 'It doesn't matter.'

'Oh, it doesn't matter!' Stephan laughed loudly. 'You are funny, you! You have a special way of looking at things. Well, and then? Go on, go on!'

'He told me,' said Marya, 'that I mustn't have anything more to do with you, or see you when you came out of jail. But I longed to see you. Because I thought it would help me. I was awfully unhappy. Oh, awfully. But when you'd gone to Amsterdam, you know, and I met him he . . .'

She stopped, passed her tongue over her dry lips, swallowed.

'He chucked you, hein?'

'Yes,' said Marya. 'He said he was disgusted with me. And that he had a horror of me and that when he thought of me he felt sick.' She stared unseeingly with the eyes of a fanatic at a little pulse that was throbbing in Stephan's cheek just above the jawbone.

He passed his hand over his mouth.

'*Quelle saleté*!' he said, '*quelle saleté*!'

Then he laughed and said:

'*C'est bien boche, ça.*'

She went on: 'It wasn't that that I wanted to tell you. Because really, you see, it doesn't matter. I wanted to beg you to be good to me, to be kind to me. Because I'm so unhappy that I think I'm going to die of it. My heart is broken. Something in me is broken. I feel. . . . I don't know. . . . Help me!'

'You must think I'm Jesus Christ,' said Stephan, laughing again. 'How can I help you? What fools women are! It isn't only that they're beasts and traitors, but they're above all such fools. Of course, that's how they get caught. Unhappy! Of course you're unhappy.'

He began to walk up and down the room.

'My poor Mado!' he said, and again, 'My poor Mado!'

'Help me,' she said.

But when he tried to take her in his arms she shrank away.

'No, don't touch me,' she said. 'Don't kiss me. That isn't what I want.'

He looked at her in silence, then shrugged his shoulders, poured himself out a half-glass of rum and said:

'Wait a bit. Where is the letter you told me you had from Heidler?'

He took it from her bag.

'So, now . . . Wait a bit . . . He seems to have forgotten that you make him sick. Well, that sort of feeling, it comes and it goes. Everyone knows that. He wants to see you? Well, now you have a place for him to come to. It's not very chic, but still. So you will write to Heidler that he comes here tomorrow afternoon. Go on, write now! And I'll post the letter. He's made a fool of you – but he forgot me when he did that. Wait a bit. I'll be waiting for him when he comes. You want me to help you. All right!'

'You must be mad,' said Marya. And to gain time she added: 'And do you suppose, if you have a row up here with Heidler, that the concierge won't call in the police at once?'

'She won't,' answered Stephan, 'before I have had time to break his back.'

'You won't break his back as easily as all that,' said Marya.

'No? Well, we'll see. I think I'll have a little advantage because he won't expect me. I'll jump on him from behind the door. He won't even have time to make a row.'

'You must be mad,' said Marya again.

'Write the letter,' he told her. 'Write it now and I'll go and post it.'

'No, I won't.'

'You poor thing!' he mocked. 'You poor thing! You have no blood, you. You were born to be made a fool of.'

'Leave me alone,' she said. 'I might have known that you'd only hurt me worse. I was crazy to tell you.' She began to cry. 'Oh, God, why did I tell you?'

'Well,' said Stephan with contempt, 'stay here and cry. It's all you're good for. I'll go and find Heidler myself.

After all, it'll be better like that. Look here, d'you see this? A revolver, yes. You didn't know that I had it, did you?'

He put the revolver back in his pocket, muttering:

'He thought I was well put away behind the bars. Wait a bit!'

'No!' said Marya.

She was standing near the door; she spread out her hands to prevent him passing.

'You shan't!' she said again. And then: 'You think I'd let you touch him? I love him.' A delicious relief flooded her as she said the words and she screamed again louder: 'I love him! I love him!'

He muttered something, collapsed on the broken armchair, and sat staring at her with miserable eyes. He looked small, shrunken, much older.

'You left me all alone without any money,' she said. 'And you didn't care a bit what happened to me. Not really, not deep down, you didn't. And now you say beastly things to me. I hate you.'

She began to laugh insultingly. Suddenly he had become the symbol of everything that all her life had baffled and tortured her. Her only idea was to find words that would hurt him – vile words to scream at him.

'So,' he said when she stopped breathless, 'now I know. Very well. As you like. Now will you get away from in front of that door?'

'No!'

He gave an impatient click of the tongue and caught her wrist to swing her aside. She fought him wildly, with frenzy.

Now, added to all her other terrors, was the terror of being left alone in that sinister, dusty-smelling room with the enlarged photographs of young men in their Sunday-best smirking down at her.

'You shan't go, you shan't! I'll call for the police. If you go out of this room I'll go straight to the police-station and give you up.'

She saw the expression in his eyes and was afraid.

'No,' she said piteously, backing away from him. 'I didn't mean. . . .'

He caught her by the shoulders and swung her sideways with all his force. As she fell, she struck her forehead against the edge of the table, crumpled up and lay still.

'*Voilà pour toi*,' said Stephan.

He straightened his tie carefully, put on his hat and went out of the room without looking behind him. He felt dazed and at the same time extraordinarily relieved. As he went down the stairs he was thinking: 'The concierge; I must be careful of the concierge.' But the concierge's *loge*, when he passed it, was in darkness.

Outside in the cool street he found himself face to face with Mademoiselle Chardin.

'*Tiens*,' she said, 'good evening you . . . I left my bottle of scent upstairs; have you seen it? Is your wife there?'

'No,' said Stephan, 'there's nobody there.'

She looked sharply at him, took his arm and asked what was the matter.

'Why, nothing,' said Stephan, beginning to laugh. 'Nothing at all. I am looking for a taxi. I'm going off.'

'Take me with you,' said Mademoiselle Chardin suddenly.

She had a very pretty voice. She thrust her hand into his arm and walked along with him.

She repeated: 'Take me with you, Stephan.'

'But I tell you I am going off,' said Stephan. 'Off, off! I'm staying one night in some hotel near the Gare de Lyon. Tomorrow morning I'm off.'

'Exactly,' said Mademoiselle Chardin. 'As it happens, I know a very good little hotel around there. Comfortable, not expensive. We'll talk.'

A taxi crawled past them. Stephan signalled to the driver.

'I'll take you there,' said Mademoiselle Chardin.

She climbed into the taxi and, leaning forward, gave the driver an address in an authoritative voice. Stephan hesitated, climbed in after her.

'*Encore une grue*,' he was thinking.

At that moment women seemed to him loathsome, horrible – soft and disgusting weights suspended round the necks of men, dragging them downwards. At the same time he longed to lay his head on Mademoiselle Chardin's shoulder and weep his life away.

She put her warm hand over his firmly and said:

'My little Stephan, don't worry.'

The taxi rattled on towards the Gare de Lyon.

JEAN RHYS (the name is Welsh) was born in the West Indies and went to England when she was sixteen. Encouraged by Ford Madox Ford, she began writing in Paris during the 1920s and published five books before World War II—*Left Bank, Quartet, Voyage in the Dark, Good Morning, Midnight* and *After Leaving Mr. Mackenzie*. In 1966 she wrote *Wide Sargasso Sea*, the story of the first wife of Mr. Rochester of *Jane Eyre*, which won the coveted W. H. Smith Award in England.

VINTAGE CRITICISM,
LITERATURE, MUSIC, AND ART

VINTAGE BELLES—LETTRES